Chris Wilson is a full-ti
the Department of Con
London.

By the same author

Baa
Blueglass

CHRIS WILSON

Gallimauf's Gospel

Paladin
An Imprint of HarperCollins*Publishers*

Paladin
An Imprint of HarperCollins*Publishers*
77–85 Fulham Palace Road,
Hammersmith, London W6 8JB

Published by Paladin 1991
9 8 7 6 5 4 3 2 1

First published in Great Britain by
The Harvester Press 1986

Copyright © Chris Wilson 1986

The Author asserts the moral right to
be identified as the author of this work

ISBN 0 586 09091 6

Set in Baskerville

Printed in Great Britain by
HarperCollinsManufacturing Glasgow

All rights reserved. No part of this publication may be
reproduced, stored in a retrieval system, or transmitted,
in any form, or by any means, electronic, mechanical,
photocopying, recording or otherwise, without the prior
permission of the publishers.

This book is sold subject to the condition that it shall not,
by way of trade or otherwise, be lent, re-sold, hired out or
otherwise circulated without the publisher's prior consent
in any form of binding or cover other than that in which it
is published and without a similar condition including this
condition being imposed on the subsequent purchaser.

For Fiona

Let not the man who is beast or who thinks he is God come near me.

               Louis MacNeice

The characters of this story are my pale fictions. They do not resemble similar people who are their own inventions.

1

In the Penal Colony

Chattering crazily, the beast moves upon them. Soon he will trespass, naked and frisk-footed, across the threshold of their lives, etching his shadows on their minds. The dazzle of his darkness will swallow their light, for the moon shall eclipse the sun. His shrill laughter will seduce their daughters, his antics pervert the sons. Then he will taunt and tease the parents. He will befriend the evil and subvert the good. His sardonic gaze will penetrate all secrets. He will know and awake their lusts, then teach new ills. The people will be drawn helplessly towards him by the suction of his sin. When they recognize him for devil, and try to cast him out, he will remain – more dangerous in spirit than he ever was as flesh. Prayer shall not save them.

'Everything is in order. Everything has its true and proper name. Jahvy has arranged it so . . .' The Parson Lovegrave paused, greedily sucking back the trickle of spittle that leaked through his bloated purple lips. He menaced the lectern with taut red hands and scowled downward to confirm his revelation of the divine will. Assembled before and below him, properly ordered to a pattern of their power and privilege, are the good folk of Iffe. The two rows of pews are for the gentlefolk. The first is for the men of importance. We can count three of these. The merchant Hogg is gross beyond the call of fatness. As if mocking him, Doctor Gallimauf sits long and stiff, lean beyond any sensible proportion. Between them, the embodiment of healthy compromise, Thomas Hooker, bailiff, strokes his pock-marked chin. In the row behind are the women and children possessed by these good men elect of Jahvy. Taking precedence, for she is cousin of Lord Iffe, Mistress Hooker sits on the right. Alongside, her three sons are ordered in descending scale by protocol by size. At the other end of the pew is Mistress Hogg and her daughter Cordelia. The space between the two families is for the wife and children of Doctor Gallimauf of whom there are nonesuch. The kindly scholar has no helpmeet. Looking back over his shoulder, he sees the space that speaks his solitude and is skewered on a shaft of sadness.

Behind the pews, distanced by deference, huddle the rest of the congregation — fishermen, labourers and their families. The rain that fell on them as they trod their ways to church now rises again as steam from their hunched woollen shoulders.

Two people are missing; the highest and the lowest. Lord Iffe of Iffe has an intimate relationship with Lord Jahvy of creation whom he entertains alone at home. Mad Vera, idiot, sprawls lewdly, legs splayed to the wind and rain on the granite steps of the church. She looks up to the timbered doors closed against her. She knows her place which is without.

'Jahvy saw that man was lonely. As man slept, Jahvy drew a splinter of bone from man's foot and made woman. And he called her woe-man. From man's foot she comes and there she belongs. She shall bruise his heel . . .' The Parson spoke with rising frenzy and smeared his oily, ginger hair back over his bald crown. Some vanity seized him as he spoke to woman of woman. Even now she titillated. From his perch in the barrel pulpit he could see down to the thighs thrusting themselves brazenly through thick woollen skirts. He imagined the legs of Cordelia twitch, beckon and spread. The Parson saw the languorous hairs on the precipitous slope down from her belly. There were coral lips around crimson lips that throbbed open to yield the tunnel of wet corruption. But her eyes denied all this and she looked up in coy pretence of piety.

'Jahvy placed the pig above the chicken, the horse above the pig. To each he gave a position in the order . . . To each group he gave a king to rule. Jahvy said let the eagle be lord of the birds, the whale be king of the fishes, the lion king of the beasts. But above all these he placed woman, and above her he put man, as the eagle rises above the sparrow. Let there be lords and labourers and let each know his place and be content.'

The front pews shook and creaked rhythmically with the bouncing of Hogg's thighs as he tapped his feet in irritation.

May a man not improve and enhance himself, thought Hogg. Is a lord nobler than a merchant, Lord? Am I not like the good beer, with dregs below and froth above? Am I a lesser man because I work and prosper, neither resting like a lord nor lazing like a labourer?

'. . . each man's place is fixed because it is given by Jahvy. Does the thistle pretend itself an oak? Does the herring believe himself a porpoise?'

Does the Parson believe himself? Doctor Gallimauf's eyes flickered closed in exasperation, then sealed shut in pleading prayer. Must I rest rude and stupid as your vicar, Lord, who speaks but cannot hear? You have blessed me with five most excellent books. I know them. Now I need another. The door to knowledge is closed against me – locked from the other side. If you cannot send me sensible company, Father, best send me a book instead.

'This world was paradise. Each from worm to seraphim had his place and knew it. The light shone all day and it was warm. There was neither famine nor disease.'

It may be, thought Gallimauf, that you created me, Lord. Or else that I imagine you. Perhaps we are both phantoms in the Parson's nightmare, purple pigments of his ramblings. The possibilities are infinite. Faith finds cover in curious crannies. It might be McGuigan's goat who is truly the Lord of creation. How ashamed we all shall be, having tugged her udders so often to steal her milk so long.

'It was always mid-day. It was ever summer. There was no labour for Jahvy had made everything in proper order, in proportion for the needs of each. Yet things are not so now.'

Parson Lovegrave paused to glare at the congregation and felt his outrage resonate in echo through the timber of his lectern. 'Man has sinned. He has tumbled and the earth trembles beneath the clatter of his sins.' He scowled first below him, and saw Gallimauf wink in reply, then threw his head back to focus his distaste on the poor folk huddled behind. 'Now there is labour . . .' he told the labourers, fixing them with a gaze of contempt that they should know that work was their doing.

'There is disease.' Lovegrave's gaze pierced Mother Fox who looked away, shame-faced. Her cheeks were bloated and blue – for she suffered blue-bloat – and her arms were twisted at unlikely angles to her body.

'There is misery.' He stared at Smith the smith whose wife had drowned four days before. Washing clothes in the tub, she had tumbled in. The container was too narrow for her to turn right way up as Jahvy and gravity intended. For this double affront to the natural order – of inverting herself whilst impersonating some fish – she had been taken slowly from this world, her long struggle visible only by the thrashing of her soles and heels on the surface of the tub.

'And there is madness.' The Parson pointed a strong stern arm to the church door on the other side of which, it was known, knelt the Mad Vera. She answered through the door with an extended scream of pain. 'She cannot enter. We do not know her and will not see her. No man may call to her for the church has reclaimed her name.

'There is pain and labour, poverty and lunacy because man has tumbled. It is man's work not Jahvy's, our doing not his. You have made things so. You sin and make the land shudder . . . You upset His order. The woman that Jahvy made rose from man's feet, tempted him to lie with her. Man's parts met woman's parts and there was corruption, vile corruption. In remembrance of this are women cursed and caused to bleed . . .'

Then, sir, there is the matter of my daughter. While we are on the issue of women, I must tell you this. Hogg could not prevent a tone of peevishness from tainting his thoughts. My daughter can find no husband, sir. She is a rose, bursting into bloom in the favour of your Providence. Yet what man of substance and property may claim her before the petals fall? Do you mean her to grow over-ripe, then wither like fruit unclaimed? You have given me a jewel, Lord, yet you tease me by withholding a market. Is her talent to remain hidden beneath the bushel of her spinsterhood? Having thus reminded the Lord of pressing business, Hogg opened his eyes to consider bride prices and the premium on a maidenhead.

'Jahvy so loved man, he sent his son to try us and teach us sternly. Grist said let many be drowned for their guilts. Some he had hung by their necks or ears, others were thrown from windows. A few were turned to salt or had their bowels drawn out. Those that were not too wicked for saving were spat over the lands and islands. So our father's fathers were cast like spittle on Iffe . . . that a life of proper suffering might lead them nearer to the paths of Jahvy.'

Mad Vera lies face downward, spread-eagled on the steps. Her cracked red legs thrash the stone as she appeals to Jahvy over the head of Lovegrave.

'I was a baby once, Lord, and suckled by a loving mother though I cannot remember her shape or name. You gave me a baby myself. I nursed and loved it, Lordy. Then they took it away because of the devils inside me. Then the devils gave me a babby. Then they took it away and kilt it. Take them devils out of me, Lordy, before they take my tongue and use my parts for their naughty works . . . Smelly Vera need to love. Jahvy and Jahvy virgin help Vera unugly. Gristy help it? . . . Pweskilly, paltrify, Verabody, Lordy?' she pleaded. 'Give it Vera's story. Prayer body Vera tryful stilmost, heartfull Vera goodbusy, godshit, Grist piss . . .' and she wailed and tore at the soiled shawl around her neck as if to strangle herself.

'Yet Grist shall not be mocked. As you plant so shall you harvest. Jahvy shall write his laws in the blood of men and smear it clear and large with their entrails . . .'

The Parson told them of the terrors of the judgement, that

in their fear they might find His way. But he was cruelly visited and tempted by passions of flesh. He thought of women. Of pink and brown and scarlet parts, moist and dry parts, of lean and fleshy parts, smooth and wispy, hard and soft, breast and thighs, lips and grooves, tongues and juices. Often, as now, the parts were not those of his mistress wife but those of woman in the general or another in the particular.

'The fire we know is as ice compared to the fires of Hull. Yet Hull does not end. A single breath in Hullfire, as the flames fry the flesh of sinners, is stretched to the time of a life on Iffe. A single scream lasts one hundred years. There will be no hope, nor any end.' The Parson hesitated and contemplated his erection with sour pleasure. Sacramental wine trickled down the belly of Cordelia Hogg from the spring of her navel. The host was held moist in the cleft between her spread thighs.

'Pray that Jahvy may find the ring in your nose and pull you like a stubborn beast from the mire of temptation to the stable of his grace . . .'

Vera has left no trace. Her stains on the step have been washed away by the rain. Now, kneeling behind the briars, she chews nettles and watches the congregation stumble out from the church. There is nodding and bowing and quiet sombre speech. Daniel's boy laughs but is silenced by scowls.

Today is Jahvy's time, but tomorrow the beast will come.

2
Pan Troglodytus

Perhaps it is a crucifixion. The figure is flat black against the unclouded sky except for the sparkle of gold on its chest and around its neck. It is suspended upside-down, fifty feet aloft, held to the sprit by a single bent leg as though nailed through the knee. The arms hang down straight and limp from the shoulders. As the ship rolls the figure stays plumb and true to the tyrant gravity. It seems a dead and broken body, oddly misshapen and disproportioned. The arms and legs look stretched, the torso swollen, the neck compacted, the head flattened. Now it shows life, bending with lethargic grace from the waist. The torso rises and the arms reach upward to grasp the sprit. The legs drop and splay apart. The body jerks in spasm, pumping out a golden stream which falls like a curved rod of glass to the deck, striking with the crack of a whip lash. A sailor struck by rebounding spray looks about him startled then screams his reply,

'Your mother was an ape and she fucked a baboon.'

The figure above, now swinging by a single arm, shrieks its delight then breaks into cackling laughter. It is a well-tried joke but always brings a fresh pleasure. Sailors stay their busy, mechanical fingers from the patching of sails, raise their eyes, join the raucous laughter. They take sides.

'Piss back, Jacques.'

Tired by its show of wit, contented by the acclaim, the figure aloft returns to a relaxed posture, wrapping its legs over the sprit. It closes its hairy lids to the mid-day glare and snuffles happily.

There is taut order here, for this is a ship of war. Each has a position in the chain that reaches from the heavens to the keel.

The captain responds to the revelations of the weather and passes its commandments to the mate who in turn instructs the crew. There is a surgeon to sever limbs shattered by ball and shot; to discern between the dead, the dying and malingering; to stop the lash at the fatal margin; to shave and manicure the captain.

The cook boils salt mutton, boils soup, boils vegetables, and serves raw the sailors' daily wage of spirit.

Above all these is a masterless spirit. Perched in the rigging lazes Maria, the cook's monkey but her own person. Her tasks are many but not onerous. She pisses from the rigging, scratches herself, takes exercise, gives amusement through her naïvety and cunning, is ornamental, brings luck. She is wealthier than most, acting as banker for her master cook who decorates her with booty. There is whim, love but also sense in this arrangement. It is difficult to part an ape from its ornaments. Around her neck is a gold chain in which is mounted a central ruby. She wears a blue felt waistcoat, gold-buttoned, held tight at the waist by a leather belt with an ornamental silver buckle.

They sleep together, the cook and Maria, sharing warmth, dreams and a hammock. As the cook lies drowsing, Maria may be seen leaning over him, gently fingering the strands of his hair. She hunts the flea. She holds the insects with some delicacy in front of her nose, as if myopic, to examine them before nibbling them affectionately – gently popping their firm shells to suck their crimson juices. The impression of fiercest care is not misleading. Both parties are scrupulous in serving the other's needs. This ape eats better fare than the captain and has a key to the brandy cupboard. She, for the cook, is an entire family: a naughty child in need of a father's firm direction: a confidante brother for bouts of maudlin drinking: a comforting mother with a loving touch: companion wife in the velvet dark of night.

She is six years old now, nearing full size and a mature

wisdom – the veteran of two campaigns and uncanny exponent of the crafty arts of survival. She would anticipate the arrival of shot, running screeching moments before it struck. Now her cowering presence in battle made the men brazenly foolhardy, whilst her shrieking departure left them chilled in dread. She was a lucky soul, blessed by Providence. Her presence brought a favour to the ship. For this she won respect tinged with reverence. In consequence, her manner showed a definite confidence as if she were impersonating an alderman.

Though shorter than a man, she is almost as heavy and decidedly stronger in kick and punch. She is not to be trifled with. She will not suffer monkey business. A sailor once hid her accustomed spoon and passed her a fork with which to eat her potato soup. She'd scrutinized the implement with pleasure and curiosity, then tried it. She noted its failure to grasp the substance of a liquid, eyed her tormentor with deliberation, then hurled herself upon him. It had taken three men to pull her off and the best part of a jug of brandy to soothe her.

She isn't one of those who becomes raucous or violent when drinking. Rather, she is fey and gentle, stroking her companion's back or fondling his hair. She listens to a man's problems with sweet sympathy and care.

Were it not for her lack of conversation, her habit of sampling her neighbour's plate, of stowing unwanted food in another's mouth, of gargling with her soup, one could introduce her to the highest tables of society. By the standards of the crew, she shows a fastidious refinement of manner. At dance she enjoys a Bourrée or Gavotte. She is most precise and elegant of step and can either lead or follow. When we see her face, we understand that she understands. It is as if she has seen the world before this life. In restful contemplation her features show that she has tasted the weakness, deceit, cruelty, treachery or indifference of others and has chosen to forgive.

Hers is a broad, furrowed forehead above a long bony brow. Her dark, recessed eyes gaze with steady wisdom. Truth is held like dirty fluff in the creases of her cheeks. The nose is strangely small and delicate above bulbous jaws. The lips are wide but thin. In all, she seems more than human.

Now she feels strangely troubled, swinging from perch to perch but finding comfort nowhere. She looks out to the west and sees grey clouds gathering, congesting the sky and filtering out the sun. The sea is frothed and foam-flecked. She whimpers a feeble protest and slithers down the mast, passing Pierre-one-foot who rises to hitch a sail. They trade only the briefest grunts and strokes for each has a hurried purpose.

On deck she scuttles from side to side, peering to the sea which rises to the level of her face, flinging its waves at her blinking eyes. Sniffling in pain and shivering she hurls herself through the galley door where the cook is boiling his soup. She throws herself upon her friend, seizing him two-handed around his back and toppling him against the wall with the weight and ferocity of her ardour. Nuzzling his right cheek, she squeezes the cook for love.

'Merde, Maria.' He pats her head then forces her away, returning to his steaming cauldron which swings madly as though about to escape its fastenings. Maria tugs at his arm to lead him out on deck but is clipped round the ears for her pains. Whimpering, she scuttles out on all fours. It comes at her too fast this barrel, careering down the hill of the deck to take her for companion. She grips it with both arms as it strikes her chest and clings to it as if to her mother as it sweeps from the side of the ship. Screaming and chattering, she holds to the rim and scurries ever faster to remain on the barrel and out of the sea.

The sound crushes all others, surrounding itself by stillness. Like the scrunching of bones or a howl of despair, it is heard in the bowels not the ears. It starts hesitant then soars in assurance, a long, ripping, splintering crack. Sailors can only hear this once. The mast trembles then wilts, across the deck and over, tilting the ship into the hug of waves. Then the boat rolls over and waggles its green keel to the grey sky.

3
Flotsam

There was a radiance through the mist as the barrel came to rest, rocking only slightly as the waves lapped it with a new softness. Maria found she could stand, and released from the efforts of holding a precarious balance, began shivering and chattering with cold. The shower had softened to spray and she began to dry in the cold breeze. Salt formed silver and grey along the filaments of her fur and as a crystalline scab on her face. She stood, rocking the barrel beneath her feet, but it resisted her force as though clutched by hidden hands below.

Gradually the world began to form to her view. At first, she could distinguish only a sinuous white line in the distance, dividing the greys of sky and sea. Then she saw this snaking length as the threshold of beach beyond which were the lazy curves of hillocks fringed with grasses. Suspicious and cautious, she lowered a leg. As her knee met the water, sand formed around the arch of her sole. She jerked back the leg with a howl of protest and rubbed and slapped it until the warmth returned partnered by prickling pains. She knew she could reach this land but loathed the chill water and the treacherous touch of the sludgy sand.

Now safe, she turned her mind to miseries. There was cold and hunger, thirst and cruel solitude. She scooped sea to her mouth then spat it back howling. It was stronger than the choking taint already locked in her mouth. She had known anyway. This water was clear and chill not warm, milky yellow like the good ship-water.

She rocked herself, grasping her legs tight to her chest, making the smallest shape she knew to the biting mouth of wind. Then, opening her eyes again, to risk a quick look, she chattered excitedly. This land was moving towards her. Lowering a leg, she found the sea reached only to her shin. Soon this land would come to claim her.

She knew land and its powers – how it sucked ships towards it and held them firm and tight like the hug of a friend. It had a curious stillness and forgot to shake a person. It was the home of fruit where a cook lazed all day in the arms of his friend.

With the shore only paces away, she leapt from the barrel and scampered up through the shallows from wet sand to dry. But something held her. She turned plaintive eyes back to the barrel and went back to roll it laboriously up on to the beach. Turning it on end, she sat upon it and swivelled through a circle so that she could better survey the scene.

At first she was unsure. The dark shape on the hillock fluttered at its edges as the wind rustled her own fur. Then she saw it to be a person like herself; for, whenever Maria looked towards it, it quickly knelt as though believing itself then hidden. So she turned away to seem distracted, whilst holding the figure at the edge of her sight. It dropped from view then bobbed up again to peer out from the top of a close mound. It would come in its own time – and with it, food. People held food.

This one was shy and cautious, not like those she'd known before. The sand had brightened to a sharp yellow before the figure presented itself on the flat of the beach. There it stood, perfectly still but for the flutter of its black shawl, gazing at Maria. It turned its back and whistled then turned to look again.

The day was growing old and still there was no breakfast. It was the nature of people to ignore her needs. Maria reverted to a display of studied disinterest to hasten the figure's approach. It moved around Maria in slowly decreasing circles with a stumbling walk, as if drunk. Stopping in front of Maria, a few paces away, it goggled and gaped at her face.

'He's so ugly,' said Vera. There was rapture in her voice,

radiance from her face. 'Such an ugly, bow-legged, hairy man for Vera, Jahvy be praised . . . What's your name, ugly body? What word do they have for you?'

Maria shivered and chattered. Hanging his head on his shoulder, he rolled his eyes pitifully and pushed two fingers into his mouth.

'Dumb,' pronounced Vera, divining more than she'd heard and examined this stranger with enhanced warmth. 'I shall call you flotsam, because you are washed ashore as helpless as kelp . . . as pretty as a sea-slug . . . useful as a jelly fish . . . Do they laugh at you, flotsam? Ugly, dumb, cripple, because you are so hairy? Do they throw stones or use the nettles of words?' Mad Vera reached out a slow and gentle arm, fluffing the hairs of the stranger's neck. 'They call me Mad Vera,' she explained, 'Elvira is my name and mad is my rank. There are devils inside me. They take my body and use it for sin. They wander through my thoughts and unpick my reasons. They are sleeping now.' Vera lowered her voice to a confidential whisper, 'We must be quiet as cod so as not to wake them. They are fallen angels and lacking bodies they borrow mine.'

Maria considered the proffered hand of friendship. He reached out quickly with irritation, prodded Vera's palm then pointed two fingers back into a gaping mouth.

'Hungry, flotsam?' Vera reached to her bosom through many layers of cloth and sacking and withdrew a blotched, wrinkled potato. The stranger seized it, pushing it whole into his mouth. Closing his eyes in the fiercest concentration, he chewed passionately, swallowed, reopened his eyes and gazed expectantly, beckoning with a frenzied hand for more. From her shirts Vera withdrew a partly used carrot past its prime. On renewed demands she was able to find, in the more intimate recesses of her clothing, a knob of bread, two more potatoes, a fish head, some flaccid cabbage leaves and an irregular portion of an apple.

'Poor, starving, ugly, bow-legged, hairy, bedraggled beggar. Vera look after you. Won't let them sniggle and laugh. Keep you hidden. Give you food that the devils steal for Vera.' She took him by the hand and led him across the beach and over the dunes.

'Vera's house,' she said proudly, pointing to the gorse bush draped with sacking. She showed him the tunnel through the prickly foliage but he seemed not to know the qualities of a door.

'Vera show you, dumb flotsam,' and she crawled into the bush along the hollowed trench of sand. Looking back over her shoulder she saw the stranger stoop to look in.

'Come in, hairy beggar. This is our home.'

They huddled in the cavern of the bush, Maria arched over Mad Vera, running his fingers through her hair, lethargically picking off fleas. Shielded from the sharp, damp wind, sharing their misty breaths, they rest. His belly swollen by breakfast, with Vera whispering her kindly abuse, he responds to the ache of his limbs. His head drops to rest on her chest. His eyes close. He snorts and burbles contentedly.

Vera draws open the layers of her shirts to lay bare her left breast. He nuzzles it, his thin pursed lips quivering and bubbling on the heaving, wrinkled slope. Vera wraps her arms around his neck to hold him tighter. Wriggling briefly, to find comfort on her pliant contours, he moans gently. Then Vera knows from his snuffling snores he is asleep and entirely hers.

4
The Nature of Hats

'Jahvy be with you, old man. May your parts never wither.'

'Grist bless you, young man,' the old man raised his blind and rheumy eyes as if to see. 'Do you know the portion of the day?'

'If the day were a glass of ale, old man, only a third part would be drunk. There would be froth still and the dregs would not have fully settled.'

'Then Daniel has milked his goats?'

'He has, old man. But he hasn't yet beaten his son. The boy has still to chase the Parson's dog.'

'The boy is stubborn.'

'The boy will not learn, old man, nor will the dog. They are links on a chain of ignorance.'

'Dermot has set his pigs to the acorns?'

'He has, old man. They are snuffling, burrowing and wallowing, except for the old sow with the blue ears. She has pushed through the hole in the hedge and is eating Daniel's seed corn.'

'Then Martin has watered the milk for market?'

'It is done. The goodness is lost and it is ready for sale.'

'Then Mad Vera has run weeping, wailing and tearing her hair?' The young man paused and his brow puckered, 'Now there is an ado, old man. She has not. Her time has come and left without her.'

'Ah,' the old man sucked his gums and nodded, this proved his suspicions of the world. 'It is a misshapen, deformed day, a sorry cripple. It is spiky and bent like a bramble, not straight and true as a willow. The days are growing more bent. The bends become twisted, the twists get knotted. There are hands afoot that pull things from their proper shape.'

'This may be so, old man. Your blind eyes see things that are hidden by light and sight. They say you know all the colours of black and every shape of the night.'

'I see things I would rather not,' said the old man. 'Things get worse as they decline.'

Maria had been gazing down at the men as they spoke and had slowly eased down through the tree. Now she lay along a branch, an arm's length above their heads. They had neither gun nor stick and seemed at peace. Slowly, she reached down and gently lifted the woollen cap from the old man's head. She sat on the branch, sniffed the hat cautiously then placed it on her head. Both men looked up.

'Who is it?' asked the old man in a tone of weary grievance, 'who hides in trees to steal the hats from the heads of old, tired, blind men? Is it Daniel's boy?'

'It is not. This is a stranger. He is hairy and dark-skinned. He wears a waistcoat over black goat skin. He raises your hat to you to wish you good day.'

'If a golden light surrounds his head, he is perhaps an angel.'

'There is no light, old man.'

'Or else he is a devil come to make mischief and tempt us with sin. What will he offer for my soul? Make the sign of the cross and ask him his name.'

'He returns the sign of the cross, old man, but does not speak his name.'

The old man raised his eyes to the tree. 'I am an old, blind man with only a single hat. My name is McGuigan, perhaps you've met my goat. May Jahvy bless us both and lead us from sin. I wish you health, wealth and good fortune, and as many hats as you desire. A blind man with but a single hat cannot afford enemies and must needs be a humble friend of the world. My hat, as you will see, is but a poor old thing like myself but nonetheless I value it. Perhaps, when you have enjoyed it a moment, you will return it me. It warms the chill thoughts of an old man. It is the brother of my hair and the best friend of my head.'

The young man reached up to receive the hat but the stranger leapt back along the branch, holding the disputed hat to his chest in the passion of possession. He bared his teeth in a wide grin and chattered nastily.

'He smiles, old man – like a friend – but he does not return your hat. His words are foreign and twisted. He is not of our sort. Perhaps he does not understand our ways or the nature of hats.'

'I've heard words like his before,' said the old man, 'on the larger island across the water they speak like that. They twist the proper sounds of words so that they become like bent spoons that cannot carry. The meanings slide off the edges, fall to the floor, and all is a dollop of nonsense.'

'I will teach him the truths of Iffe,' and reaching up the young man began to shake the branch on which the stranger sat. But Maria was unperturbed, looked down calmly then casually climbed upward until he was lost to view behind the foliage. Nothing was seen or heard of him until an object dropped from the heights, rebounding from branch to trunk to earth.

'It is a button,' said the young man, holding the object to his teeth to bite it. 'A gold button. The stranger has paid you for the hat.'

'My trousers are of the finest wool,' McGuigan spoke in a wheedling tone as he stared blindly up at the tree. 'They are barely stained except at the front and rump and are but three winters old. Pay me what you will for them, sir. I am a blind and stupid man. I trust to your judgement of the fair price of clothes.'

'These boots are extraordinary,' the young man competed for the stranger's ear. 'You might happily stand knee high in pig shit for the whole of Lent, should you wish it, and not feel the slightest damp or chill. The secret, sir, is in frequent greasing with goose-fat.'

* * *

Daniel's boy had crawled through the long grass to watch the men and gazed bewildered. He turned and ran home, unwisely and unusually to tell his father what he'd seen and done. 'Old McGuigan and Angus Brodie are standing under the old oak by the river. They've taken all their clothes off, father, and have lain them on the ground . . . their dingles are hairy and they're talking to the tree . . . what does it mean, father? Come and see, come and see.'

Daniel listened to the boy in patient and resigned silence. Then, for the second time that day – for a father's work is never done – he lifted him by the collar and slapped him fiercely about the ears in his tender concern for the boy's morals.

5
Elements of Semiology

It is a well-known truth that an epistemologist, following erratically in the steps of Poxmire, and a monkey, travelling without particular thought of arrival, will find interests in common when their paths cross. So it was.

They approached nonchalantly enough, pretending disinterest, then paused some yards apart and scrutinized each other. Gallimauf raised his fleece cap. Maria doffed her hat and shook it with such exuberance that the scholar suspected some irony or parody. He felt it impolite to betray his surprise but Maria had no such reservation. She ran her eyes up the scholar's length as though he were some livestock in a sale, chortled as she scanned his impassive oval face and found special pleasure in his evasive, darting eyes.

This is no peasant, thought Gallimauf. He has the arrogance of the merchant class. I shall replace my hat and stare him back. He shall not patronize me.

'Good day, sir. You are perhaps a stranger here?'

'Huch . . . cha.'

'Yes, sir?' Gallimauf gazed with expectant interest but couldn't coax any further words. 'Perhaps we might walk a little way together and pass the time of day. I am Gallimauf the philosopher . . . perhaps you know my treatise.'

'I take you in my confidence, sir, because you are a gentleman and because you too must know the barbs of ridicule. You have a noble ugliness, sir, a feature you share with Socrates together with his suspicion of eloquence.' Perhaps I am too intimate, thought Gallimauf. He makes no sign of sympathy. Maybe he shuns the Socratic tradition.

'I am the bastard son of a kettle. My life has not been easy. I have had to bear ridicule. Jocularity has attached itself to the conditions of my birth.' Gallimauf looked sadly to his feet and blushed. 'I tell you this because you also seem a man apart. I mean no disrespect. You are a man of dignity and bearing. There is deep wisdom in your eyes. Your ugliness is quite compelling. I just suggest that there is affinity between us when we find ourselves amongst the simple folk of Iffe. We understand each other, do we not? We are men apart. We are different.' Doctor Gallimauf smiled at the stranger and met an unblinking stare of profound wisdom from those brown, recessed eyes.

'My mother . . .' the doctor continued, 'became pregnant by an unknown hand – I resort to a proper delicacy here . . . My father remained concealed, my mother refused to reveal him. There was much talk. Some blamed the church, others implicated the Lord Iffe, but my mother stayed mute. Thrown from her father's house she wandered the paths and fields, finding food and shelter where she might, growing weaker as she became larger. Finally, she bore me premature and still-born in a stable, then promptly expired herself – from shame, hunger and exhaustion.

'There I might have ended, before I'd begun, had they not sent for the good doctor Gallimauf. This kind man, learned in Biologics and the movements of the humours, clutched me in a sheepskin and bore me to his home. Placing me in a kettle above his hearth, he basted me in nourishing liquors and broths. And there, above his hearth, I completed my term and incubation. The day came when he peered through the steam that rose from the pot and found me ready and fully formed for the world. Immediately, he summoned the midwife to ladle me pink and steaming from the pot . . . For clarity and convenience, I count that as my true birthday and the good doctor as my father. And this . . .' Gallimauf stopped in his tracks and withdrew a polished kettle from his leather case, 'This, sir, is my mother.' He held the pot with scrupulous care and introduced it to the stranger. 'We must count our blessings and through the alchemy of our optimism transmute misfortunes to joys. Providence shines on me. Though father has died, mother is ever at my side.' And with a caress to her dented polished curves, Gallimauf returned his parent to the custody of his case.

'So you see, sir, I too am different from the common man. As a man of tolerance and learning, I know the narrowness of vision, the blinkers on the heads of men. There are those who suppose that, because they wear red braces, the Lord Jahvy suspends his trousers likewise.' Gallimauf laughed alone. Perhaps this stranger was a dangerous democrat who thought that men were equal.

'They presume that if they eat boiled cods' heads so does the Holy Spirit. They confuse their own habits with truth, sir and regard their own appearance as the natural condition of man. I know, sir, with education they would see as us. But from their pit of ignorance they snigger at the sky. I must warn you. Your trust in the common man may be misplaced. I think they will laugh at you. They will observe your legs and comment on the lack of trousers – assuming that tubular leggings are moral armour. They presume a sixteenth commandment – "thou shalt wear trousers". Whilst they know from familiarity the hair of the scalp, they will not comprehend the luxurious growth that so ennobles your neck, chest, arms and feet. For they do not realize, sir, that Jahvy has given you such an exuberance of fur to protect you against the chill wind of colder climes. The people here are good, we know. But they lack experience. They do not realize that the Lord has painted men in a range of hues from his broad palate to ornament the world. Imagine how much greater their surprise if you were a yellow body of the Chinas or green person of the Antipods. They lack your profound and contemplative silence, the people here. Their words rush ahead of their thoughts till the two are quite lost from each other. Do not be offended, sir, if they mistake your elegance for strangeness.'

This is the oddest and rudest of men, thought Gallimauf, and grotesque as a gargoyle.

'It would be my privilege if you allowed me to act as guide. I know all people of consequence here – not only the bailiff and Parson but also the Lord Iffe. I am respected as a man of learning, scholar and physician. I can read, sir, without moving my lips one fraction. Though this, as we know, is a trick familiar to several philosophers. I own, sir, five books.' Gallimauf released a self-deprecating whinny then promptly strangled it. The stranger made no reaction except to rock gently, fixing the doctor with a steady, curious gaze.

'When I say own, I mean know. I have read each of these books to such a pitch of familiarity that I am now ready to acquire a sixth.' The stranger raised an eyebrow in gesture of dismissive contempt. He thinks I am braggart, then I shall show him erudition, Gallimauf decided.

'I have been much influenced by the *Treatise* of Muirpocks of Broosk. He writes, as you will know, that we do not exist. He denies us personal identity, saying there is nothing so constant in our experience as to prove the continuity of self. I make no secret, that I regard this merely as his personal supposition. Yet if it is so, then he does not exist and we need heed him no further. I aim to write and publish this refutation. Then those unfortunate enough to have met his insidious book may be reassured of their existence, identity and property. It also seems, sir . . .' Gallimauf grew louder in outrage, 'that Muirpocks denies the existence of miracles – though his grounds for doubt are themselves doubtful.' The stranger nodded in time to the metronome of the doctor's wagging finger.

'I have been concerned also with the writing of Doctor Lakuna who claims that the consciousness of man has the structure of an omelette, which is a badly fried egg. This is a more difficult fallacy, more tricky to expose. I know, sir, I know . . .' Gallimauf pointed a stern finger, ponderous in emphasis to stop the man from interrupting. He would have his say. 'The error may be to take as unified the phenomenon of consciousness as refractory. Is being not an accomplice of the totality?' The stranger nodded his assent without much show of surprise or interest. The point, it seemed, had occurred to him already.

He shall not diminish me, thought Gallimauf. He shall not make me feel the yokel. I am a scholar. I know five books. Perhaps there is one of these he has not read.

'You will know, of course, Monsieur Bath's *Elements of Semiology: Sumatran, Runic, and the other tongues of foreign bodies.*' This, apparently, was a rhetorical question for Gallimauf didn't pause for reply. 'He argues that we only know the world through the window of our language. Since different peoples have different languages, they know different worlds, such that when they meet communication is impossible. In support of this, he shows that some tongues lack words for yesterday, for sausage, or even for Jahvy. He further proposes that there is nothing so particular or apt about a word that another might not do its labour as readily. We might call Jahvy "sausage", as long as everyone so agreed.

'I know this to be so from my own research . . .' Gallimauf leaned towards the stranger and lowered his voice to a confidential whisper.

'For two months now, I have been calling my parrot "dog", and my dog I have rechristened "parrot". There was an initial confusion, I admit. Both were bemused for some days. But then . . .' Gallimauf was breathless with excitement, 'the bird and beast adjusted — unruffled by their reversed names. And despite this change of language, there is no discernible change in their habits or their natures. The dog it is who barks. The parrot still shits on my manuscripts.'

The stranger narrowed his eyes and creased his brow.

'No, sir, no. That is not it.' Gallimauf smiled his triumph and shook his head. 'I live alone. The consistency has not been caused by other folk continuing to call them by their former names.'

As their eyes met, the stranger chortled approvingly and raised his upper lip to expose his orange teeth.

'Good, sir. You find some elegance in my proof . . . I notice that you follow the line of an argument with great sagacity and rigour. You nod assent or disagree. But you are reticent, sir, in speaking your own opinions.'

The stranger confirmed this by his continued silence.

'You are not vulgar or raucous in imposing your views on others. But I worry, sir, lest your discretion may be motivated by a concern that you cannot fully trust me. Be assured, I am liberal, quite liberal. It is my view that between scholars any manner of supposition is permissible. There must be no walls to discourse, save those of honesty.'

But still the stranger was mute, returning the doctor's darting glances with a steady stare, stroking his jaw in serenest contemplation.

'Should you wish to discuss Adam's navel, or the carnal practices of angels, I should not be shocked. No matter should be hidden from the scrutiny of scholars.' The hairy man remained attentive but mute.

Another idea was forming in the doctor's mind. 'I am slow, sir, not to guess it sooner. It may be that whilst fluent of ear, you are silent of tongue. Have you taken a vow of silence as servant of Jahvy? If this is so, you might give me a sign.' But the man's manner did not alter. He gazed knowingly and scratched his thighs.

'I know, then, sir. I have guessed you out.' Gallimauf's voice rose to a higher pitch and trembled there excitedly. 'You are a foreign person. Your language is otherwise. I shall loosen your tongue, rest assured. As a student of Doctor Bath's, familiar with each of the two hundred pages of his excellent monograph, I know the tongues of foreign peoples . . . You are Sumatran? Or speak the runes? Gallic? A Mongol?

'Quantum est canis in ille fenestra? . . .

'Pidatko sinna ampiaisista? . . .
'Varuum leerlaufreaktion? . . .
'Je est un autre . . .

The stranger leapt back through a full circle then jumped up and down clapping his hands above his head. He shrieked and fell into a forward roll.

'Au premiere est que la semiologie, bien qu'a l'origine tout l'y predisposat, puisqu'lle est langage sur les langages, ne peut etre elle-meme un meta-langage.' The doctor continued, smiling broadly to have finally diagnosed his companion. 'Then you are a Frenchman, sir.'

Trembling and chattering, the stranger climbed on to the doctor's lap, nuzzled his ear and stroked his hair. 'It is unfortunate, sir, though I know some profound quotations of the masters, there are so many meanings I cannot say. But let us strike this bargain. You teach me your tongue and I'll show you mine. At the end of a month, sir, we shall talk of the essence of essences.'

'Huchahuchahucha . . . huch,' declared Maria, pushing her rasping tongue into the scholar's ear whilst holding him locked in a fierce embrace.

'Huch, huch,' conceded Gallimauf, squirming, 'Mais il faut cultiver votre jardin.' But he knew there was more to the matter than that. The flick of that mucoused, muscular tongue in his ear had released within him a dizzying tumult he could not name.

6

Sins of the Ears

They assembled not by arrangement but by unspoken understanding, not at the parsonage but in the inn. The concerns as yet were secular.

'French, a Frenchy man.' Gallimauf bawled in the Parson's ear. The reverend gentleman, though deaf, did not suffer deafness. He recognized his disability as providential and fitting. His task was to talk not listen. Sealed ears spared him the distractions of conversation and tittle-tattle. He was immersed in the refreshing sea of silence. Hearing, ever since deafness first struck him, had seemed a perverse and dangerous practice. 'The ears,' he observed, 'are Satan's gateway.' Though he had a fierce denunciation for each and every bodily part, and was damning of appendages, he reserved his fullest fury for the orifices and senses. Ears, as those most perceptive of holes, earned the gamut of his wrath.

'I believe he must be a Frenchman,' the Parson Lovegrave announced to the others. 'This has been revealed to me.' He frowned as he considered his disturbing news. 'They say that the French are a hairy and uncivilized race, much obsessed with their prongs of generation which are the devil's digits . . . Satan sticks his fingers wherever he can. The French are complicit in many heresies. Some deny that the son is coeternal with the father. They assert that Jahvy made the world not from nothing but of his buttocks. Some Frenchys claim that the soul of Grist died with his body but was then resurrected . . . But there is worse – a heresy I mention only to men of your discretion. It is claimed by some men of France that it was not the son who died on the cross but the father – and that he never rose again.'

'It is not my turn to buy the beverage,' said the merchant Hogg looking morosely at his empty mug. 'It is the Parson's turn to buy for us. The Lord sealed his pockets when he plugged his ears.'

'Why yes, sir, thank you,' the Parson smiled at Hogg, 'put the poker to the ale and let us warm ourselves some more. We must think upon the Frenchman and caution charity with care.'

'He is a wise and careful man,' said Gallimauf. 'I raised the issue of Adam's navel and the carnal appetites of angels. He protested loudly by his silence that he would not trade in heresy. He is scrupulous in basing his ideas on a thorough reading of the Book. He will not admit the existence of the phoenix. A solitary bird may not exist since Jahvy's creatures entered the barge by twos. We spoke of the ladder of creation. He concurred with me that there may be forms of life as yet unknown. We agree to suspect the plausibility of a form of being to tie the link between man and beast. Likewise, he agrees the chance of life on a higher globe to complete the chain between lords and angels. It may be that they have designed carriages that allow them to fly to meet us. If so, their sexual organs will be vestigial – for they will reproduce themselves by thought . . . This much the Frenchman has told me but there is a barrier to our intercourse,' the scholar reddened and sipped some ale, '. . . though the visitor understands our tongue, he barely speaks it. My mastery of French is still incomplete. However, in our friendship and to aid our disputation, we have sealed a bargain. Each will teach the other his tongue.'

'You are inebriated by your head, doctor,' muttered Hogg, 'your thoughts are blind companions to your mind. Do not let them lead you. Spare logic and tell us what matters. Does the man stay long with us on Iffe?'

'This depends on the progress of his affairs.'

'They say he is fair and proper in Trade, paying promptly

in gold. Does he have partners in Commerce? Is he master of a vessel, merchant or agent?'

'He is solitary in Trade. He arrived alone. His boat is gone. We did not talk of business but spoke entirely of those matters of philosophy that tickle his curiosity. For a man of Commerce he is curiously well versed in the philosophies of Muirpocks.'

'It is known he has come to purchase hats.'

'He has interests in hats,' said Gallimauf, 'but they are not his sole concern.'

'He is a married man?' asked Hogg.

'He wears no ring and makes no mention of a family. My understanding is that he is a single man, continent like myself.'

'It is rumoured his manners are not ours.'

'He observes the customs of his nation as is proper for a patriot,' Gallimauf spoke with rare irritation in defence of his friend. 'Instead of shaking hands, which is most curious and arbitrary, it is the custom of his kind to finger another's hair. In registering surprise or joy it is the convention to perform a backward leap in the air, completing a full circle before regaining the feet. The French are singular in their agility, as is witnessed by Doctor Lakuna himself who stands on his head whilst conversing in Greek. It is sometimes their habit to hang from one arm by the lintel of the door while holding conversation. The stranger is affected by a childhood accident that has hampered his gait. He stoops with a hunched back, so that when he walks his knuckles may even scrape the ground.'

'He is hairy beyond the call of manliness.'

'Indeed?' Doctor Gallimauf resumed a reproachful severity. 'It is my experience that each man is hairier than others and less hairy than some. That much is told in the Book of Jahvy.'

7

The Third Philosopher

'Shit,' said the parrot in a tone more pained than angry, 'the parrot has shat on my manuscript.'

Doctor Gallimauf ignored this counterfeit of his own currency being swept on the tide of his reverie. He was infatuated.

Piqued by this inattention, the parrot strutted along the mantelpiece, kicking aside the jottings and quills that lay in his path. His eyes were ablaze, his feathers ruffled. 'Pestilent bird,' it shrieked. 'Pestilent bird.'

But the doctor was not distracted into reply. He was a man preoccupied and besotted, could think of nothing but the stranger – wanted nothing but the Frenchman. He was lost to lust. His desires were precise, fierce, rude and carnal. He wished to penetrate the fleshy brain of the stranger, thrusting shafts of inflamed meaning through his ears, 'How wonderfully we are fashioned for such a consummation. My flesh has lain virgin for such a scholar. How pink and darting his frothing tongue! How fleshy and pendulous the lobes of his ears, around the hidden orifice.'

The kindly, reticent scholar has fallen prey to unnatural passion. His parents were to blame. Whatever their other merits, the philosopher and kettle were deficient as guardians. Despite the wisdom of the one, the domestic utility of the other, they were lacking in love. Mother did too little. Father did wrong.

To use his mother as cooking pot had always seemed improper. Her value to the boy, then, had been her passive metal presence. Malicious gossip whispered that she was tarnished copper and called the kettle black. But to her son, at least, she was good as gold and radiant as the moon.

Each parent has a tested solution to the perplex of emotion. Gallimauf senior always chose the counter-punch of reason.

'I love you, father,' said the boy.

'Really, boy? The concept is opaque to my view. Do you mean eros or agape? Do you lust for me or love my being? You might perhaps explain yourself. Or should you prefer we might debate Hekel's four proofs of the translucence of angels.'

So the boy had grown to find intimacy and beauty in scholarly disputation. When his adoptive father passed prematurely on – victim of the mismixture of his disordered humours – the young Gallimauf was left with none on Iffe with whom he might express the affections of epistemology, the lusts of logic. He had been forced to disputing with himself, finding prompting echo in the recitations of the parrot. So persistently did he question and answer himself, and on such repetitive lines, that the parrot had mastered the themes of debate.

'How do I know that I truly exist?' Gallimauf demanded.

'You cannot, sir,' he told himself, 'and in posing the issue in those terms, you needs assert what you seek to question.'

'That is the shallowest sophistry,' Gallimauf was outraged by this travesty of his position, 'and you will not let me finish, sir, you are forever interrupting.'

'But you said "I" sir,' he instructed himself.

'I did not. Or, if I did, it was as a hypothetical entity . . . besides, you said "you" which proves my point.'

'Muirpocks can refute this,' the parrot advised.

'Did you say that?' asked Gallimauf. 'Or was it the parrot? I was not watching and could not see if his beak moved.'

'It was not the parrot,' said a voice not unlike his own.

'Pray stop imitating me,' demanded the parrot, 'you are ever intruding upon my discourse.'

Had the good doctor researched the carnal potential of persons, he might now find useful precedents for his designs upon the Frenchman. He wished no more to excite himself but yearned for another's body. There would be need of courtship, sly evasions, coy words, stealthy approach. At the outset, there would be need of a pretext.

'I will go find the stranger,' he told himself, 'I will speak honestly of my passions. I shall bare my soul. When he knows my love, he will yield.'

'Above all, one must doubt everything,' declared the parrot vaguely.

'You are a beast, sir, and a heaven.' Gallimauf rounded on the bird, which fled startled to the highest perch. 'When I wish to crap through the airs, I shall consult you . . . Or should I ever choose to pass an egg . . .' He spoke with icy cruelty. Throwing off his bedclothes, he donned his Sunday jacket and considered the issue of breeches. Without my trousers, he mused, I shall be as he and that will be a gesture of friendliness. Yet, I may not find him but meet all other manner of folk who will laugh. Conventions may often be arbitrary, but if there is no cost one can readily accept them. In the long term, it is preferable that we both wear trousers. But I shall not force him. In time he will respect the convenience of leggings. Or he might go unclad at home while we write our manuscripts, and be dressed to convention when we venture forth to greet the world.'

Rushing from the parlour, with Muirpocks' *Treatise* beneath his arm, he slammed the door of the cottage. He had forgotten even to say goodbye to his mother who lay abandoned upon the chest, casting her golden light on the whitewashed walls of the parlour.

He was exhilarated by the rashness of his plans. This was the moment he had awaited – when a man of ideas finds the purpose to become a man of action. As proof of the pudding of his passion, he would loan the stranger his copy of the *Treatise*.

8
Hogg's Cross

The merchant sat immobile considering his possessions and the responsibilities that Jahvy had laid upon his shoulders. Amongst his burdens was a weakness and discomfort of the legs, caused by swellings, brought on by a sensitivity to wines and fine foods, exacerbated by a healthy appetite. As a result, the merchant required the four legs of two bearers to compensate for his own poor stumps. When he moved on business, as now, he was carried in a sedan chair – unless the terrain was steep or confined, in which case the porters took turns to bear him hoggy-back. He had tried a horse but found it less personable, responsive and tractable. Besides, he knew from scrutiny of accounts, a single horse eats more oats than two men.

Gazing imperiously down the mound of his chest, over the summit of his belly, beyond the fence of his gold watch chain, he felt an envy for his porters who, though his match in years, had a vigour that cannot be bought at market. He yearned to cripple them with his growing weight of flesh and looked eagerly, each fresh day, for signs of new weakness, breathlessness or fatigue. It seemed a cruelty and irony that he, elect of Jahvy, was crippled whilst they should scurry with such unflagging energy.

'The cross I must bear through life . . . a heavy one . . . is to be borne on the backs of others.'

The sense of injustice was dispelled briefly as he noticed that all within his view belonged to him – fields, sheep, bearers, lake. But raising his eyes to the skies he was reminded again of his finite powers.

'Let us walk past my wood, up to my river and watch my geese.' He saw with pleasure an expression of resigned pain flit quickly over the face of the elder bearer. 'We need our exercise.'

Looking back over his shoulder to the right, Hogg saw his house in the distance and winced. Time was complicit with the elements in assaulting the propertied class. Even now, drops of rain, as those gathering to miniature torrents to descend the slopes and twists of his face, were wearing rivulets on the facade of his home. In a further year the house would need refacing. The mortar would need replacing between the stones by servants whose flesh was weakening and would need replacing by Hogg whose own strength was waning slowly. And the wind blew in disregard of his possessions – rattling the tiles of his roof, lifting some from their fastenings, scattering the petals of his roses, laying his fine rich soil on the Lord Iffe's fields, hurling back the Lord Iffe's grit upon his fragile window panes.

These are the burdens of wealth and duty. Jahvy had lain upon him the tasks of possession and denied him the soothing balm of ignorance sprinkled so copiously on the poor. Life was battle against unrelenting time and decay. There could be no victory but only slow defeat, delayed by stern defiance, perpetual vigilance, continual repair.

'We are tired now. We have walked enough.' Spheres of sweat broke loose and down from the merchant's brow, 'We must hurry home to the demands of Trade.' The porters swung around and trotted more briskly. They are like horses, thought Hogg, who returning weary from the hunt suddenly frisk at the smell of their stables, the sight of home, the prospect of oats. Hogg brooded on the burdens of his office. These men could rest now, by pretending to busy themselves at some menial task, while he must continue to rack his mind for solutions to the paradoxes of Trade and anticipate the vagaries of the Market.

Foremost on his mental Ledger was the Account of Cordelia. He had invested unselfishly in his daughter for sixteen years now, without thoughts of Return or Interest. But now was harvest time. Yet where was the buyer for her blooming crop? This was a perishable stuff, being neither smoked nor salted and very much alive. She was a plum verging on ripeness. There was an iridescent bloom to the skin, a firmness that would soon swell to succulent softness, a slight sharpness that would yield a gorgeous sweetness. From then there were the sickly and pungent processes of decay.

'Run,' he shrieked to the porters as they entered the lane to his house, 'time shall not wait for us. We have the urgency of Business.' He was tormented by the vision of a barn stacked to the rafters with over-ripe fruit – turned to yeasty rot, sellable only to fools.

Lowered into his chair in the parlour by the bearers, Hogg clapped his hands impatiently. Mistress Hogg, Cordelia and the two spaniels – Outlay and Return – formed in a line before him.

'We will sit ourselves. We have family Business to discuss . . .' The dogs wandered lethargically to the hearth and lay themselves down. The women curtsied, then sat. Cordelia dropped her eyes and resumed her needlework. Mistress Hogg clasped her hands in front of her chest and smiled modestly at her husband.

'We wish no more than our daughter's happiness,' Hogg pronounced, then paused, distracted by the ceiling. He gave a disciplinary scowl to a wooden beam to scare it from its inclination to warp and split. 'We wish her to graze contentedly in the hedged pasture of murridge. We have considered suitors and have been disappointed. There is Gallimauf, but . . .' Hogg hunched his nose in distaste, 'he is poor as a field mouse and crazed as a squirrel. He reads and writes, which distracts him from truth. When nature moves him, he discovers his part with surprise and pisses into the wind. We think he is the only doctor who has failed to note the discrepancies between men and women. Or if he does know gender, he finds there no interest or importance . . . He cannot please our daughter for she would wish for a man. She would want less than philosophy but more than idiocy. Such a murridge could bring no benefit to our family and could not satisfy our child . . .

'Our Lord Iffe we know looks favourably upon our daughter, often and from every side and distance. Unlike the good doctor, he knows the differences between men and women but does not see them cause for wedlock. He employs women servants at all times of day and night. The people of Iffe so admire their Lord that they cause their children to wear his nose . . . He has a laxness of mind that causes him to forget. Being forgetful, he forgets he has forgotten. We know to our cost, his costs are low. Having proposed that earnest contract of murridge, he might forget that he has done so. Should he remember so far as to murridge her, he might forget she is his mistress wife. Our Lord has such poverty of memory he grows rich on the proceeds . . . But who else is there?' Hogg looked to his daughter who looked to her sewing. If it were not for a flushing of her face and neck, one might have thought her deaf as a parson and innocent of sins of the ears.

'A visiting merchant has come . . . A man of our class. He is pious and proper. He carries gold. Gallimauf counts him as friend – that can be used and then corrected.'

'Father?' Cordelia was hesitant and shy as she spoke. 'How does he look?'

'He is of middle years, carrying wisdom and experience . . . and a mature belly. He's vigorous in mind and body. His bearded features show his intelligence. There is much energy to him. Fortunately, he is not flamboyant or excessive of beauty.' Hogg spoke warmly of the virtue. It was a feature he showed himself. 'Beauty decays. It is a corrupt base for partnership and affection. While it lasts, it leads to an excess of feeling. It undermines the equable trade of murridge. It corrodes composure. Besides, it is well known that handsome men are vain and, forgetting their vows of fidelity, follow their privities from bed to bed. We cannot allow our daughter to marry a man whose face plots to betray her.'

'Does he talk well, father? Does he make men laugh?'

'Being French, the man has a curious tongue. It is quite unlike our own. This too would benefit our child. Murridge is a long voyage. When a couple speak too much at the start, they proceed too fast and grow sated or exhausted for the latter portions of the voyage.'

'His skin?' asked Cordelia. 'Is it smooth or pocked?'

'This is hard to discern since he is dark and rather furry. The effect is very manly. His smell, though strong and curious, is not at all unpleasant.'

'And his manners, father? Is he a gentle man?'

'Being a foreign body, he does not behave just as we do. The ignorant might think him odd because his customs are French. He is used to the woods, so fond of trees. Some of his habits are casual. He is quite relaxed. All this shall be remedied. He'll quickly learn our ways. He is confident and assured, which speaks to his credit.'

'And his clothes, father? Does he dress finely? Does he wear wig or hair?'

'His hair is very much his own. Though it is thin on the scalp it is rich elsewhere. He wears fine gold, which speaks his wealth. His clothes are few and untidied by travel. We do not speak of his breeches . . .

'We advise our daughter. We do not tell her. She shall meet the stranger for he will come eat with us. He shall see the nobility of our family. We shall assay his mettle. We shall test his sensibilities of Trade and not ignore his morals. There will be roast pig's parts, pickled cods, much cheeses, many puddings and most conviviality. Our daughter's pleasure is the prize. This return justifies the risk of high Investment. No Expense or effort is excessive. We shall spend days in preparation – polishing the silvers, instructing the servants, preparing the fare. Rest assured, wife, you shall have the fullest co-operation of my counsel . . .

'And now I shall retire to my chamber. Send for the men that they may bear me to bed. Follow on, wife. We wish for conjugal privacy. It is the second Thursday of the month. It is time for you to lie on me and reaffirm our murridge.'

* * *

His panting at last subsided, recovered from the exertions of duty, Hogg raised himself up against the bolster and opened the large ledger entitled 'Being the Account of Murrital Trade'. After entering the day and time, he wrote with slow deliberation, mouthing each word as he wrote it . . .

'Gave unto mistress wife best portion of hour in guidance of her tasks and conduct.

'Retiring to bedchamber did give her, in further fulfilment of contract, in fourth position, five full squirts of myself, paid in best seed.'

9

Lord Iffe's Wits

Those who attended their Lord Iffe were unsure. Perhaps their master was unable to arrange the fragments of his past into the sensible shape of a life, or else he was unwilling to sap his energies in the needless labours of memory. It was vexsome and confusing. There were some things that their Lord always remembered – that he was master of the island, summoner of servants, seat of passions, consumer of flesh, food and wines, generous host to stray and passing pleasures. Many aspects of the world, though, and especially those unrelated to the comforts of his person, did not alight in his mind or adhere to his reason. But on occasions he would chance upon the finest and most delicate fragments of past and trivial events – disconcerting his servants by interrogating them on these splinters, demanding to see the block from which they came, insisting that the past should account for itself. Then, the master parted the present and loitered with suspicions in the intricate maze of recollection. Sometimes he cannot extricate himself; sometimes he cannot enter. His wrath, like embers, flares, then subsides to a dull glow. Within moments of releasing a scorching fury he may mislay his anger, or else sheepishly forget its cause – lost in another arm of the maze.

'Good morning, sire.' The bailiff smiled with sly unease as though he knew much more than the master. Iffe raised his head from the pillow, held a sheet protectively to the level of his chin and peered at the intruder with bleary belligerence. Then, as if he had mislaid a thing of value, the master began a thrashing search beneath his bedclothes.

'Why am I alone?' asked Iffe.

'My lord is often alone in the morning. People often rise before him.'

'Pass it,' the lord waved his hand vaguely, 'pour me some. Then explain yourself. Who are you to enter my chamber and accost me like a familiar?'

'When the master wakes fully he will see I am his bailiff, Thomas Hooker.'

'You are?' The Lord Iffe's tone betrayed a grudging acceptance of this information, or some doubts as to the certainties of his confusions. Then, as if remembering, he smiled at the bailiff. 'You have a mother, Hooker, a crippled mother with bloated ankles. Is that not so? Confirm you have a mother, Hooker, that I may know it is you.'

'Yes, sire.' The bailiff spoke wearily.

'And tell me, Hooker, how is your fat and ugly mother with bloated ankles?'

'She is dead, sire. She died three years ago.'

'Then I must tell you, Hooker, you have no mother.' Lord Iffe's tone spoke resigned reproach. 'Why did you not tell me of the death of your mother? She must be replaced, Hooker, do you understand?'

'It is done. Widow Walker has taken charge of the kitchens.'

'Widow Walker,' Iffe sucked appreciatively, 'does she have hair the colour of barley straw and a mole on her left breast?'

'Her hair is golden,' the bailiff said. 'But I am not privy to her chest.'

'That is as it should be. Pass me my gown, then go. I cannot lie abed to talk of breasts all day.' Iffe was contemptuous but the bailiff loitered on.

'As your bailiff, sire, I must warn you of the stranger. What should we do about him? Shall I have him watched?'

'Stranger? What stranger?'

'A Frenchman has arrived, without a boat, without apparent reason. He wanders the island. He talks and perhaps he plots. He listens, perhaps he incites. His ways are strange. They are not ours. He is a foreign body, sire.'

'I will advise you then, Hooker.' The Lord Iffe rubbed the

stubbly skin held taut over his hollow cheeks. An impersonal smile lit his face. 'Do not play cards with him. The French cannot be trusted at cards. They drug their horses also. Do not wager on the Frenchy's races. Do you understand me? However, at dance they are most adept. Their trousers are most elegantly cut. I commend the wines of Bordeaux. The cheeses are rich. But you must take care after dark on the roads.'

'What shall I do about the stranger, sire?'

'Stranger?' Iffe's eyes returned from the distant pleasant vista to the bailiff there before him. 'Stranger? What stranger?' The smile was crushed by a grim scowl and his voice curdled. 'Why did you not tell me? Strangers may often be dangerous.'

'I told you, sire, of the Frenchman.'

'That cannot be so,' Iffe concluded, testy with logic, 'otherwise I should have remembered.'

'Sometimes . . .' the bailiff was weary in resuming a familiar line of defence, 'when a man forgets, he forgets he forgets.'

'I do not employ a bailiff to teach philosophy, nor a cow to lay eggs. Go, and remember my instructions. Summon Widow Walker to come to me. She is the woman with the blonde hair and the mole on her chest.'

And so the bailiff left. The sly smile had returned to him. He first gave a message for Doctor Gallimauf to come bleed the Lord Iffe, then hurried to the kitchen to eat breakfast of duck eggs and beef with the friendly Widow Walker.

10
Concupiscence

'Good morning, sir. This is a fortunate meeting.' The Parson Lovegrave held out the tails of his coat as he lowered his wealth of buttocks to the stone wall of the sheep pen. He squirmed, thrusting his pelvis back and forth, until he found a sympathetic liaison between flesh and stone. 'I carry the blessing of Jahvy and some necessary guidance.' Comfortably seated, the Parson raised his eyes to gaze sternly at the stranger who sat on the lowest branch of the oak.

'Huuuch . . . hchchchuucha,' the man chattered uneasily and raised his upper lip, disclosing a curve of matt ochre teeth.

'It would be better if I spoke and you listened.' The Parson was peevish. 'I have other souls to guide besides yours, sir. The devil moves fast and furtive. I must hurry on if I am to keep pace and cancel his counsel. Besides, I am not a listening man. Jahvy has fashioned me to lead his flock, not listen to their braying. My ears are sealed to aid me in this task.'

The stranger fell obediently to silence, rocking apprehensively, holding a hand across his eyes to shield him from the Parson's glare.

'I must warn you, sir, against concupiscence. We know your intentions. You seek the hand of Cordelia Hogg. Take care lest your imagination lead you in pursuit of other parts. Murridge is a sacrament. It is not to be defiled by carnal lusts. The vows of the man are to take the woman, forsaking all others, lend her the guidance of his wisdom and enter a contract of care. This is not a libertine's charter . . . It is no licence to ravish, fondle, suck, stroke, thrust, lick, heave, wriggle, writhe – to sink in the mire of concupiscence.

'The parts of man and woman may meet, within the sanction of murridge. But this is not an excuse for pleasure, sir. On that route lies squalor and sin. The Lord Jahvy watches man and woman in their private moments. He notes, sir, and he counts. He eyes their couplings with disgust. He wishes that man and woman should cage their passions, not besport themselves like animals in rut.'

Leaning back against the tree trunk, pulling her thigh hard to her chest and swivelling her knee, Maria was able to suck her toe. At the same time, whilst holding a precarious balance and continuing to watch the Parson, she entertained ideas. Scratchit, suckit – it occurred to her – suckit browny, nicey, sucky, chewy nicey, salty, salty, spittim baldy, self-body swaffly, scratchit moresome, suckit sorebit.

'Once a month, sir. Once in a new moon. Do you understand me? The date and time to be decided beforehand, lest lust dictate the occasion. And quickly, mind, lest in lingering you wake the sleeping passion of your wife and lead her to complicity.'

Spittim sillybody no foodies, rubbybelly, sneezy windycoldy snufflenosybrrurr.

'There is but one natural posture for this activity, sir, as you will know from the Book of Jahvy. Plant your seed quickly, in the proper place with the unfortunate instrument provided. Neither squander nor linger. Remember that Jahvy watches.'

Climbit up here, Maria boppim, pinchim earies. Snifflebody, pushim. Morerubbit.

'Do not think your mouth can play host to a nipple,' Lovegrave shuddered at the shameful things that must be spoken, 'nor smear your wife with honey and lick her private valley . . . There are sour perfumes as intoxicate and unhinge the mind . . . Do not place things where they never belong, nor loiter if they chance there. I tell you this because I have heard of your countrymen. It is known they will not purge their couplings of lust, but wallow in their pleasures, besport themselves carnally in trees. Some, it is known, do this outside of murridge and many times each month. Others, it is said, approach their wives from behind and imitate the beasts. These practices are aweful exciting and very wicked. Take care, sir. You have wisely left your homeland. Do not reunite with your compatriots in Hull ... I shall make myself available, sir, to guide you in the particulars of procreation. I shall instruct you and your wife in springing the snares of pleasure.

'Of trees I must warn you further.' Lovegrave glared contemptuously up at the Frenchman who shuffled sideways and turned his head in shame. 'Your conduct leads me to admonish you. Each man is responsible for the example he offers. The old are foolish, the young impressionable. You are favoured by wealth and influence. With that social position, sir, comes the burden of example. It is an unnatural practice to perch in trees. Man was made to walk the firm ground, not consort in trees like ducks. Your posture is immoral, sir. I know this from my reading of the scriptures. You seek either to elevate yourself above other men, which shows the sin of pride, or to impersonate a bird, which is facetious, sir. It is to sneer at the natural order.

'Then, sir, there is the matter of your dress. You are immodest. Portions of your parts lie untrousered beneath the skirt of your jacket – suggestive and unclothed. The error is magnified when, as now, you perch in trees, requiring others to gaze up to you – as though you were above them. The sky, sir, is window to the heavens. That sight should not be obscured by the privities of Frenchmen. Your example does not pass unheeded ...'

There were, indeed, imitations. Doctor Gallimauf, scholar, had taken to reading in trees. Abandoning the good corrections of his razor, he'd instructed his face to grow a beard. An old man now lay dying of the gripe and chill for forsaking his trousers. It was known that the stranger was responsible, teasing him to undress – offering a bribe if he should present himself naked as a suckling babe. Daniel's boy had taken to hanging from trees to avoid the guidance and discipline of his father. He abandoned his sheep. He swung from branch to branch. When ordered down, he scratched himself, pissed on those below, shouting that he was a Frenchman. He imitated the stranger's crippled walk, hunching himself and scraping his hands along the ground. He chattered and grunted, pretending to speak the stranger's tongue.

'Of speech I must warn you further, sir. Whilst you do not heed the need of breeches, you seek to borrow my boots, to stand in my shoes. You discuss the Book of Jahvy as if you were a bishop. I shall not bear this, sir, for I know your country as a factory of heresy. On matters of theology, I shall guide. You shall remain silent . . .'

But the Parson himself fell silent. For, raising his eyes to the tree, with a glare he calculated as crushing, he found his congregation departed. The stranger was gone.

11
How Stories are Lost

'I will tell you no story,' says Mad Vera, 'and I will tell it to you now.' The stranger snuggles closer, snuffling in his sleep, an arm curled lethargically around her shoulder, his breath warm and regular upon her neck.

'Peoples have families. Peoples have peoples. Peoples have roofs and ownings. And do you know the besty thing a person has? It's a story. The story of your life. And other bodies join in and they share it. They help you tell your story. The story speaks you. It says how your body moves and what's why in your head. You carry on telling your story for the whole of your life until your body dies. People listen to the story and tell it to others. If they like the story, they tell you more and better. And when a body dies it still lives because other peoples tell its story. If your story is a besty story, like Grist's tale, then you live forever. But Vera's different to peoples,' explains Vera, 'she's got no story. Had one . . .' she says wistfully, 'but lost it. People don't notice her because she isn't a story. Just two words pushed together – mad and Vera. She was mad and she is mad and she will be mad. She can't be a story because nothing changes. Nothing happens. Nothing moves. Always the same. She's a boulder on the beach. Waves wash around her, peoples walk past but she stays still, dead as a rock. Barnacles grow on her. Kelp covers her. She's just a bump, always there, always the same. No story.

'She had a story once, but lost it. Peoples came in dark and took her tale, stole her story . . . wouldn't give it back. Hid it. Buried it. Nobody knows it. Those that never heard it don't miss it. Those that stole it won't tell. They pretend there never was Vera's story. "Story?" they asks and sniggle between themselves, "Vera thinks she has a story?" Vera asks for it back. "Vera want her story," she says. But no bodies give it back. She isn't a story, so they don't hear her. She just goes cuckoo.

'Even Vera don't know her story anymore, not the proper and true words. It falls apart, bits get lost, creams sometimes, but can't lift itself up to walk in words. Can't even stagger. Vera can't save it.'

Vera smiled at her companion and continued to address his heaving, burbling, sleeping body. 'Tell you why they stole Vera's story and hid it. Stole it 'cos it's an ugly story. They're in it. Ugly and wicked in Vera's story, and cruel and false.

'Vera's story like a mirror that sneaks up behind them and looks up their bums. Don't see their faces in the story, only their bums . . . Sees between their legs and up their bums. Parson's pinky's there. Lordy's arse in my tale. Takes their breeches off and lies on Vera. They likes it there. They shows their bums and Vera's story stands behind and watches them. They forget. They close their eyes, they busies their bodies, they groans and grunts like little piggies, they squirts their stuffs, they dribbles and moans. Then they opens their eyes and stands up, buttons their breeches, turns around . . . and then they sees Vera's story. But they's crafty bodies. They seen my story, seen my story seen them, seen they seen it see them, but they pretend they don't know. They just wander off like nothing seen them. Then they comes in dead of night. Sneaks up on Vera's story whilst it sleeps. They slip it into a bag and carries it off. Beats it with a stick to teach it their lessons. It moans and wails, wails and screams, but they don't care. They hide it – bury it – in their secret place but they don't tell. Vera asks them. Hello, Parson, Hello, Parson's little pinky. You's well? But Parson howls and screams and tells his story. His story doesn't know Vera's story. Never met. Devils tell rude words out of Vera's gob, take Vera's body and use her mouth. Vera's not story just devil's lies.

'You, hairy wreckage, can't give Vera her story. You don't

listen, deaf flotsam. You don't talk, dumb cast-up. Vera can't walk in your words. But Vera care for you. Look after you and give you a story. She'll tell you well in a tale and listen to you in her words.'

She strokes the sleeping stranger. Reaching between its legs, she fingers the lustrous dark hair on the inside of its thighs.

'Once upon a beach, there came a stranger. He was a special body for he was neither man nor woman, nor neither neither . . .'

It was dawn when Maria woke, whimpering from her dream of being crushed by a barrel. She squirmed from the clutch of the wheezing, snorting Vera and looked about her. There was an intricate mosaic of golden lozenges cast on the sandy ground through the foliage of the bush. Behind Vera's head lay the book prised from the hold of the man with the hot breath. He had run after her shouting – his words loud and plaintive as though he were hurt. She had tried to escape by retiring to the top of a tree, but his patience had exceeded her own. He had stood below, smiling and coaxing, falling silent briefly, then renewing his pleas. So she had swung down through the tree and dropped to the ground. She offered back the book but the man declined it. Instead, he had seized her, clasping her around the back, falling to his knees so their faces were level. He spoke long and fiercely, the ebb and flow of his breath teasing the hairs on her nose. He had tried to stick his tongue in her ear. When she finally broke from his hold, walking backwards away, he waved gently and snuffled quietly.

Now she raised the book to her face and sniffed the leather binding. She shook it by the spine so that the pages swung apart like a skirt. Disregarding the sequential intentions of the author, she began at page 111 and tried the contents –

> No weakness of human nature is more universal and conspicuous than what we call CREDULITY, or too easy faith in the

> testimony of others, and this weakness is very naturally accounted for from the influence of resemblance.

There was a dryness here, and a dullness to the taste. She was doubtful. Did people swallow this? Was it really digestible? She chewed on, then turned back to an earlier page.

> Tis commonly allowed by philosophers that all bodies which discover themselves to the eye appear as if painted on a plain surface, and that their different degrees of remoteness from ourselves are discovered more by reason than by the senses.

This second bite proved more arid than the first. It was a disagreeable mouthful, she decided, and tried to spit it out. But the words stuck tenaciously in her mouth and she picked away frantically to dislodge the clinging pulp.
 'Filthy flotsam,' screamed Vera, seizing the book, 'eating someone's story.'

12

Flesh

Gallimauf sat hunched over his table, his quill held delicately between thumb and forefinger, watching the paper turn brown then yellow in the wandering light of the draught-blown candle. 'Today I saw the stranger,' he wrote, then blew his drying breath over the line of neat script. 'He saw me.'

He jerked his quill hand back and forth in irritation. This was too bald and did not capture the event. He threw his pen back to labour, crossing out and commencing again.

'The eye and the gaze – this for us the split in which the desire is manifested at the level of the scopic plane.' He sat back and considered the phrases with satisfaction. But the thrill, what of that? Like the sliding of a wet tongue into an unsuspecting ear.

'Something slips, passes, is transferred, from stage to stage, and is always to some degree eluded in it – the gaze.'

And the door rattled with the blows of insistent passion. It was the stranger, summoned by the trope?

But it was Hogg, blue-nosed from cold, held in the upright on the step by his porters. 'Flesh,' the merchant announced, 'I have some flesh for you. I've brought you the modest portion of a mutton. It's not vulgar of size, or brazen in leanness. But it has a mature force of flavour. It's very ripe for eating.' The merchant unwrapped this meat from his handkerchief and laid it on the table next to the scholar's manuscript. Gallimauf leaned over and scrutinized the bone. A green iridescent meat was held grimly between fingers of dull grey fat.

'It's a singular piece of sheep.' The doctor prodded the

offering with an interrogative finger, then lowered his nose to sample its airs. 'I'm most grateful for the specimen and its provocation to scholarship. But in all honesty, sir, this meat is unnecessary.'

'On the contrary.' Hogg spoke with irritation, having settled himself in the doctor's chair. 'It is for you. It is a gift. You will not be rude enough to refuse it. In return for it you will guide me. I wish the loan of your sensibilities. If I did not give you, our accounts would not balance. Or you might advise me from a presumption of superiority. Sit, listen and curb your thanks.

'Jahvy instructs us clearly. What we have we must hold — or exchange for better. What we hold we must coax to grow and prosper . . . But there is a problem that teases me. It concerns the numbers of myself and their risk of reduction. When people are well fed, I buy their salt-cod. When they are hungry, I return it to them at a proper premium that rewards my wits and labour. This is correct. It observes the laws of Jahvy. My numbers increase as my ledgers mature. Yet there's an aspect of my Trade that evades the law of expansion, that defies the science of my Accounting. It concerns the wealth that is my body.'

Both, from their different perspectives, observed the assets of Hogg flesh. The occupant stamped the feet in frustration. The rest of the carcases trembled and shook in outraged sympathy.

'Here, my numbers show a failure of profit. The figures rebel and defy me. They will not balance in my favour. They are amoral, sir, subverting the ethic of profit. This is most unjust. My tradings prosper with all except my own person. I find profit in every man except myself. Now why is that, sir?'

'Do you not enjoy yourself, sir?' asked Gallimauf, his brow corrugated by concern.

'You miss my point. This is a truth of Accounting, so does not concern my feelings or passions. I will tell you an example . . .

'I labour hard, so I pay myself generously the wages of

food. I have taken to weighing my foods, then later weighing the growing wealth of my frame. But overall there is loss. I gain less than I pay myself. There is a leaking away of resources. There is a hole in my bucket, sir.'

'I can explain this.' Gallimauf smiled, 'Mirepoix has written on this issue. His theory is coherent, and the evidence compelling. I can summarize the discourse, sir. Mirepoix concludes that the loss arises because a man shits.'

'There is more to the matter than that.' Hogg tensed and reddened in exasperation. 'I am not a stupid man, sir. I weigh my dung also. For the purpose of Accounting, I consider it a portion of the wealth of my person. I place it in a proper column.'

'If it is in a proper column, sir, you are most fastidious. You surprise me. I see the rigour of your method . . . Your waters?'

'Of course, sir,' Hogg snapped.

'Then I cannot explain the loss – unless you trumpet your nose, so dribbling often.'

'No leakage from my person passes unaccounted . . . except on a certain Thursday of each month,' Hogg coughed discreetly, 'when I give to my wife. For that loss I make a proper estimate based on prior figures.'

'That is very scrupulous, sir. But perhaps you have not got the measure of every outcome. Perhaps you slobber when you eat.'

'I do not,' Hogg spat with anger, 'and I am most attentive to my crumbs . . . It is not just my weight, sir. I can show another evidence of the losses to myself. There is a further case I have noted. It is cold here, except when it is hot. When it is cold I must invest in further clothes, or shiver, or labour harder, just to keep the pleasant warmth of myself. The airs steal my heat. The winds run off with it. When it is hot, it is always too hot. The airs conspire to fry my skin. I must resort to the labours of sweating to counter this. The consequence is that I must make lengthy efforts to return as I was, and have no reward or advantage for the labours I make. I have reached a grave judgement, sir, and do not make the accusation lightly ... I conclude that the world is stealing from me. It takes more than it returns. The elements conspire to cheat my person.'

'Well ...' Gallimauf paused to allow himself time to halt a bon mot from the traffic of his mind. 'C'est la vie, hucha, as the French are fond of observing. There is this argument, sir. Man does not own his flesh, but merely rents it from Jahvy's treasury. When a man passes on, the assets revert from tenant to owner. But whilst he holds his body on the lease of a lifetime, he must pay the rent of his labour.'

'You think it is for Jahvy's sake I shit, for his sake I sweat?' Hogg's face showed pained incredulity. 'What profit can he gain from the leaks of my system? How does he Account this to advantage?'

'In your body you move the currencies of life. Your frame is a wide thoroughfare for the staples of existence. Your shit is mother, father, and godparent to a struggling plant. It grows strong in the providence of your blessing. Why then, sir,' Gallimauf smiled at the simple beauty of the arrangement, 'that plant is eaten, then returned to the world to be used again. These are the financial transactions in the market place of life.'

'I am much more than a gut, sir.' Hogg heaved his frame though it failed to confirm his observation. 'Jahvy has not made me to parent plants by crapping like a cow. This pleads a stronger counsel than yours, doctor. But no matter. If you have done your best you may keep the mutton.'

Both men fell silent while the enigma loitered on. The parrot, it was, who finally spoke, 'One must test the window of theory with the radiance of our evidences.'

'Exactly so, sir,' the parrot and philosopher exchanged knowing glances. 'We shall find the proper informations to resolve the perplex. We are not bird brains ...' Then, realizing, the doctor blushed crimson to have been so unwittingly offensive.

'How might Moixpire proceed?' asked the parrot. He was

unabashed. He bore no grudge. One should, when all manner of errors are said and done, judge a man by his intentions and forgive any untoward slips of limb and tongue.

'We might suspect that this specimen has sprung a puncture – has a further and informal orifice, unknown to himself or Biologics, through which his vital humours leak.'

Parrot and philosopher gazed at the merchant with renewed interest and respect.

'We might test for this by searching the creases and crevices of his naked surfaces for untoward openings.' The specimen wrinkled its nose and puckered its cheeks with mute distaste. 'However, the hole might be too small to be apprehended by the vigilance of the eye. In which case we could submerge the specimen in waters . . . Airs rise upwards, bubbling through the watery substance, signalling their escape. Liquids would betray themselves by discolouring the surrounding fluids. If the escape is of solids, these could be mined from the bottom or found tossed as flotsam to the surface. When we found the merchant's surplus hole, we would fashion a bung to plug his leak.'

'Water?' demanded Hogg. 'Would there not be a dangerous wetness in this experiment on my person?'

'The hazard would be lack of breath as we held you below,' Gallimauf conceded the problem, 'but you might align your mouth with the surface to blow like a porpoise. Water dissolves substances as you will know from the shrinkage of clothes that have suffered the erosions of rains. Internally, water is safe. Whatever is dissolved, is retained inside. Externally administered, the fluid is more dangerous. But the losses to a person's person are slow. Muirpocks has shown that a man dissolves at one hundredth of the speed of salt. All that is risked initially is the superficiality we know as skin. The pigments are lost first. But, with time, and the studious avoidance of further moistness, these can be recovered.'

Hogg rocked in his chair, reddening, then whistled for his porters who were lazing outside awaiting this call.

'Good evening, doctor.' There was a peevish quaver to the

merchant's voice. 'I fear you wish to sacrifice me to your science. I am loth to speak ill of anybody, as you know, sir. But your parrot is quite unscrupulous. I shall avoid any further costs to my person. I shall bid you good night.'

As the door of the cottage closed behind him, Hogg was incensed to hear a double mocking laughter from within. But the accord and complicity was short-lived.

'You are a cynic,' said Gallimauf.

'Oviparous pest,' spat the parrot, wordy as ever, even in anger.

13

Jarvie's Law

'Your depravity is too gross, your offences too extreme to be borne by the company of civilized men. Society can no longer afford you a place within its caring arms . . .' Justice Ambrose Jarvie smiled down affectionately at the three defendants huddled tight against each other in the confines of the dock. They offered a very pleasing symmetry, a metaphor for their complicity in crime. Between the weaselly dwarves towered the ruddy and stocky cowherd. So tightly were they pressed, it seemed as though the heads of the runts were tied to the belt of the cowman.

'You have been furtive and wicked in your treasons. But this conspiracy is at last revealed to the outrage of society.'

This burden of judgement, career of condemnation, was the tradition of the family Jarvie. Justice Ambrose was grandson of Lord Justice Coverse Jarvie, Surgeon of Sin, and nephew of Judge of Appeals Doxus Grist-Jarvie, Butcher of Broosk. But though he wore the family wig, Justice Ambrose had none of his family's famed severity. He was ever amiable and equable, summing up with jollity and wit, sometimes winking at the accused to belie any harshness of his words. Defendants won or warmed by this unlikely goodwill, distracted from close attention to the words, would thank him, Lord, for his goodness and his fairness, sir. Not till later would they realize that the discharge the judge had promised them was not from the life of prison, but rather from the prison of life. He was not pedantic. He did not search the statutes for a crime against which he could match the actions of defendants. He did not snare them in the weary and wordy generalities of law. Rather, he sought to coin new terms, christen new crimes to match the infinite ingenuity of sin, offering up fresh mirrors that the stale face of degradation might see itself anew. A labourer, unjustly acquitted of stealing a horse, then found himself sentenced to a flogging for Frivolous and Facetious Impersonation of the Lord Chamberlain. The accused, who knew neither of this office nor its incumbent, had stammered throughout his trial in a manner that the judge had enjoyed as skilfully satirical. A bigamist was fined for Choosing Too Often and Unwisely, then sentenced to transportation for Conspiracy to Exploit the Credulity of Clergy.

The judge knew that, since old punishments had failed to stem the tide of wickedness, new sanctions must be devised. It had been he who had set the precedents for de-buttoning, the fining of limbs, hanging by the ears, sentencing to obloquy, transportation to Edinburgh. His most singular contribution to the exercise of justice was his practice of trying defendants not individually but in random pairs. This speeded his list but taxed his ingenuity. It required him to conflate two crimes or else unearth the hidden link between them. This was a most satisfying endeavour. For though all men are guilty, they are never guilty exactly as charged.

A debtor had found himself in dock, partnered by a suspected murderer. The pair stood accused of 'a systematic conspiracy aimed at the assassination or economic murder of all good men of the realm bearing the Christian name of James . . . a crime of the most heinous magnitude,' the judge smiled at the pair and winked knowingly. 'In threatening the sacred lives of our Monarch, his nephew, the Bishop of Durham and Lord Chancellor . . . And for this, I ask that you forfeit your neck and relinquish your breath.'

In truth, the judge was scientist, striving to locate the symmetries and regularities of human conduct. He showed the rigour of this trade and was most scrupulous in typing and sorting those who came before him. He saw below the surface of detail to the depth of truth, ingeniously matching the therapy of punishment to the ill of crime. Those with freckles were sentenced to hard labour. All one-legged men were transported to Frisk. The judge had noted that all red-headed men, whatever their ostensible crimes, were prey to fierce and unnatural carnal desires. Those in whom the perversity lay latent were most dangerous for none might be safe from the sudden eruption of their unpredictable passion. 'If we brand your forehead and split your nose,' the judge confided, 'you will warn people by scaring them, thus saving yourself from sin.' Those with speech impediments were flogged, that the harsh Doctor Lash might free the rusty hinges of their tongue whilst leading them to be better people. So did Ambrose Jarvie consider the entirety of a person, murridging the law and medicine in meting a considered and considerate justice.

There stood before him, gazing up to his amiable smile, two lewd dwarves, indistinguishable twins. One had evaded payment for a pig by pretending to be the other. Between these two – Matty and Hatty Archer – stood a cowherd accused of passing forged coins. Both twins swore they were innocent, protesting they were the other. 'I am victimed by mistaken appearance,' they spoke in unison, 'the naughty one is my brother Matty.' Duly, they turned to scowl, each at the other.

'Tell me, pray,' asked the kindly judge, 'how your good mother knows you apart.'

'By my character,' they said, 'I am of good conduct, though my brother is a villain . . . He brings me trouble by saying he is me, hiding behind our resemblance, using the shield of my name. Our wife will tell the truth of this.'

The judge nodded judiciously and noted the truth of this. Both twins had brown jerkins with two red and two blue buttons. Their shirts were the same, both hacked at the collar. Both had a crescent scar on the forehead and a space at the front of the mouth where teeth are often housed. Neither was clearly not the other. Each was very much himself.

'Since I cannot distinguish you, I must trust you. If you are both Hatty Archer and not his brother Matty – who is a villain of the lewdest character – I acquit you both of the charge.'

The two smiled as the one the judge declared them. 'Yet . . .' said the judge, 'there is the matter of your complicity with your brother. In sharing a wife in grossest adultery, in failing to report his crimes, you have colluded with him, aiding and abetting him, thereby leading him to his fall.' This is just, the judge concluded, I have the measure of their problem. 'Life has not been easy, I know. Most men have but a single body, two arms and legs.' He beamed his warmest sympathy, 'Whereas you have had to share a life between two frames, with two mouths to feed for a single wage, four legs to tire as you trudge your weary path. Whilst most men speak their mind, you have been in two minds and constant disagreement. These are problems that compel our sympathy. I shall spare your life, and both your necks. I shall remedy your problem by sending you to another place where your brother cannot compound your confusion. Freed of the curse of resemblance, beyond the dark shadow of your brother, you may find peace with your consciences. Yet when your brother comes before me, as surely he must, I shall make him answer his crimes and pay his debt to you . . .'

So much for the two faces of the bemused brother. But the cowherd, how was he involved? The judge paused, struggling to find the pattern.

'But there is the further issue of the conspiracy between the two of you. You, Hatty Archer, have with you, Tobias Gabriel, mounted a conspiracy against the candour of appearances, seeking to befuddle the minds of men with the narcotic of deceit. In passing false monies, in denying the separability of men and the accountability of their conduct . . . in being two men in three bodies, you have sought to overthrow the touchstones of our trust. Yours is a treason against reason. I sentence the two of you . . .' the judge nodded, politely enough, to each of the three in turn, 'to be transported to Iffe.'

'Where, my Lord?' asked the clerk.

'Iffe,' the judge spoke sadly now, 'Iffe is not the kindest of islands, unless you be a sheep. If you have a fleece and horns, and much enjoy moss, it is not an unpleasant place, except for the winds. Men do not land there willingly. None return. Fishermen, it is known, shun its shores, preferring far the storm. It is thought that the natives, being the progeny of convicts, are less than fully kind. Go then,' the judge advised the prisoners, 'and practise your unreason there. Do as you wish, take what you will – then pay for it. If you will go forth to meet your justice, I shall retire to greet my luncheon. It is smoked eel today. I shall not pay it the insult of delay.'

14

The Signifier

The household had been in frenzied preparation for two full days. It had washed its dirty linen, cleaned behind its ears and swept beneath the carpet. Every colour of every part was enhanced. The tiles of the hall were a sharper yellow, the timbers of the dining-room a richer brown, the walls a brighter pink. The charcoal burned a more luminous blue in the grate. Hogg's face was a more radiant crimson, his linen a whiter grey, his boots a glossier black. The spaniels had emerged from their lathering having regained the spots of their puppyhood. They paced the hearth with detached sadness as though looking for themselves, sniffing their coats suspiciously as if foreigners to their fur.

Cod's livers had been stewed in goat stock. Goat chops had been fried in cod's oil. Sheep's offal had been pressed into the caverns of boiled cod's heads. Cod flesh had been mashed with the softest and most private portions of a pig. The mixture stretched a sheep's bowel which heaved and pulsed as though to vomit up its pink, ruby and orange chunks. The outer portion of the pig had been roasted. Its blood had been fermented to a bubbling, nourishing liquor. As if this were not enough, there was a pudding of barley boiled in pig milk – a delicacy usually reserved for Grist Mess.

Pretexts had been prepared. All parties had been instructed in the gestures of nonchalance. Fine details of protocol had been written, then rehearsed, that they might pass as habitual.

The stranger would sit between Hogg and his daughter Cordelia. Towards the end of the evening he would transfer his attention from the former to the latter. The piss-pot would be passed French-fashion, from the gauche to the adroit, when the women had parted the supper table. Hogg would lead the guests in the disinterested amble of conversation for a period before supper. The servants were to address their master as 'Lord Merchant', the guest as 'Your Honour'; they were to wear white ruffs and aprons. Their hair had been made tidy and glossy with pig lard and parted in the centre.

All that was now lacking was the guest. He was four farts late. Gallimauf had been sent to find and bring him.

'You are late, but we do not blame you,' said Hogg. 'I see that you have been delayed by Gallimauf.' Some misadventure had befallen them on the way. The doctor's coat was torn and flecked with mud. He was sodden from the waist downwards. His hair pointed in as many directions as were available. Someone had bloodied his nose. The same villain, or an accomplice, had stolen one of his shoes.

'We were delayed in disputation . . .' Gallimauf panted, 'on the nature of social obligation.' Hogg ignored this and smiled uneasily to the stranger.

'This is celebration. It is my birthday,' Hogg lied, 'but as you did not know, I do not expect any present except your company. We welcome you to join us as one of our family. It is a modest supper, but it is free. We do not ask you to pay. There is no cost. You are welcome as guest. Our words are too shabby to clothe the full measure of our naked pleasure. We shall drink your conversation as the finest of wines. Decant the liquor of your wisdom in the jug that is Gallimauf. He will pour it forth into the goblets of our ears. Do not fear to tax his capacity. He is not dull. He is curious as a squirrel and collects the nuts of truth. He would enjoy your company and candour even if we did not pay him – which we do most fully – for his service as translator.'

'Huch . . . cha . . . hucha,' declared the stranger, swinging his arms in agitation, eyeing the merchant with frank distaste.

'What does our guest observe, doctor?'

'Well now . . .' Gallimauf creased his brow and sought the

words to convey the complexities, 'This is a most convoluted nuance. Meaning does not reside in a single term, as the French frequently observe themselves, sir. What he means, then, is all that he does not mean. What he says is everything that he has not said. To be exact, sir . . . his greeting may be best recognized for all it is not. He has not licked your ears, which signals the warmest of friendship, nor has he ignored you, which would convey indifference. Neither has he pissed on your floor, which would express contempt for you. You may conclude, then, that he regards you with a proper and temperate affection.'

'We shall sit,' said Hogg, 'and have the innocent pleasure of each other without any thought of commerce or try at mean advantage.' He bent at the knees until he felt the seat that the servant pushed beneath him, then slumped into the cushion. The stranger looked hesitantly from Hogg to Gallimauf then hopped upon the scholar's lap. He sprawled back, reaching languorously behind him, resting the palm of his right hand on the scholar's pate. Hogg breathed heavily and dripped an anxious sweat. Things were not going as he had hoped and intended. The stranger was casual in receiving the gifts of hospitality, unhelpfully silent, disrespectful of manner. A man should try to impress a future father-in-law or court him with respect. 'He is cunning,' Hogg decided. 'He pretends he does not want my daughter. He looks for a bargain. He tries to buy her cheap. Then I shall pretend she is not for sale. We shall talk of other things.' But of what? Though eloquent of trade, garrulous of prices, fluent of negotiations, lucid of purchase, Hogg was shy with those slight and ornamental words unrelated to commerce.

Yet he must be indirect, must feign disinterest. A conversation might serve the need – one of the utmost inconsequence. To this end, he had been preparing that very afternoon: 'To what school of usury do you belong, sir?'; 'Would you say that pigs are under-priced on Iffe?' But such questions seemed too demanding for a man of such brevity. Perhaps an observation might be better. The stranger could then repay on his own terms, trading words at whatever rate he judged as proper. I reply at a premium of eleven words for ten, mused Hogg, but the French are evidently less generous in repayment. So he brooded as the pressure of silence built to a crushing force, its sharp leading edge squashing his chest, forcing his breath from him.

'I own one hundred and sixteen hogtares of land,' Hogg blurted, then blushed.

'Our friend hears you,' said Gallimauf, breaking the hurt of silence with the pain of words.

They sat mute until the pressure on Hogg's chest again forced an issue of speech.

'The weight of my flesh is sixty-five hoffles . . . Soon it will take three men to carry me.'

'The guest has noted that you are a man of substance.'

The company fell silent again, avoiding one another's eyes. The stranger alone seemed comfortable, gazing insolently around the room as if assessing the value of the contents.

'None question the virginity of my daughter Cordelia,' Hogg resumed the conversational duties of host. 'Though she is pretty as a rose and old enough to be a son's mother, being sixteen years old, she is unscrumbled, entirely unbefumbled. None doubt this. It is known to all on Iffe.'

'Ch . . . ch . . . ch.'

'What does the guest observe, doctor?'

'It is a frequent expression, sir, much used by the French. It acknowledges what has been said. As the words pass, it pays the compliment of interest or surprise. There is no exact equivalent of our tongue, but the gentleman is saying something like "Fancy that", "Would you believe it" or "You don't say, squire".'

'But I do say,' snapped Hogg, 'she is uncoffled.'

'Ch . . . ch.'

'My daughter,' protested Hogg, squealing his anger, 'is as I say. I am no liar, sir.' His knuckles cracked loud on the arms of his chair. 'Her intimate property is unscrumpled. The man fortunate enough to gain her will have untarnished ware

'... But enough of this and that. We have refreshed each other with words. Now we shall find the sustenance of the supper table.' Beneath his face, muscles laboured against impulse to build a smile, heaving the fleshy slabs of countenance to new and fresh alignments.

The stranger ate in a relaxed, informal manner in the French mode. He sucked the fingers of one hand whilst the other spooned soup into Cordelia's ear. The girl shivered, panted and reddened but kept her gaze downwards to her plate of frothy pig's-blood broth.

'What does he convey in his transactions with my daughter's ear?' Hogg feigned a slight but amiable curiosity.

'It is very profound ... The gentleman signifies this through the pun of gesture – though it is through the mouth that the body gains succour, it is through the ears that the soul gathers strength.'

'Indeed?' Hogg's tone implied disbelief. 'So why does he now walk upon the supper table? Why has he waggled his foot in the communal pudding?'

'Why, sir, this is his finesse in building wit upon pun through the savage satire of his movements. In his mime he offers metaphor. He reminds us of a spiritual realm above the physical plane of gluttony and lusts. He warns us that a man whose buttocks are ever on a cushion, whose belly props him up against the supper table, whose piggy eyes ever search for money, must abandon hope of salvation. The pudding attracts his fullest fury for it symbolizes the richest and sweetest of carnal distractions. He invites us to follow his example in resisting the corruptions of the body.'

Hogg considered these meanings for some moments then shrieked for his bearers. They held his arms as he stepped on to the chair and from there lifted a foot hesitantly to the table. With cautious tentative steps, as though treading a fine wire above the deepest chasm, Hogg shuffled forward slowly towards the pudding. He stood above the bowl of creamed and sweetened barley. With a gurgle of delight and a maddened gleam to his eyes, he dunked his foot to the depth of an ankle. Reaching out, beaming, he offered the hand of friendship to the guest. But the man jerked the proffered fingers causing Hogg to slide backwards and down upon the table, impressing and spreading the cheeses with the generous outline of his rump. From his prone position, with his heavy heaving frame decorated with food, he gazed reproachfully at the stranger.

'Why does he seize me down?'

'He is very witty,' Gallimauf smiled. 'He warns you that despite the best intentions of elevating the soul from its bodily prison, there is ever the threat of a fall. A man may find himself wallowing in the mire, besporting himself like a hog, unless he holds his spiritual footing.'

'We wish to change the subject,' said Hogg. 'We thank him for his mummery, but we have discussed theology enough.'

There was no malice to the stranger for now he sat alongside Hogg in front of the hearth, carefully unpicking, then eating, the food that adhered to the merchant's jacket.

'I cannot accept less than five cattle,' said Hogg. He showed the spread fingers of his right hand lest there should be any misunderstanding. The stranger repeated the gesture twice.

'Ten? You will pay me ten? . . . and ten sows in pig . . . and my weight in honey . . . the sum to be paid within one month of your murridge.'

'Huch,' the stranger conceded, now strangely compliant.

'And you offer also your chain and cross?' Hogg fingered the jewellery with sincere affection. As the stranger lowered his head, the cross disappeared from the world of light to the spacious depths of Hogg's breast pocket.

'As Jahvy watches, as the good doctor Gallimauf is our worldly witness, we strike a solemn bargain.'

The man shook Hogg's hand and then his leg, completing the affirmation by pressing slippery lips to the merchant's cheek.

'Then you are my son and I your father.' Hogg's appendix of generation rose hard and proud against his trousers, as always when consummating a good bargain. He might have extracted an even higher price from this credulous stranger. But he was satisfied. A grateful son-in-law would benefit him more and further.

'You will not wish for courtship. It is our practice on Iffe not to tease a lover. I shall instruct the Reverend Lovegrave.'

15
Devil's Warnim

The devils are stirring in Vera, fomenting anger, spluttering and dribbling, venting their mean spirits. She scratches the left side of her face, sinking the nails deep into her skin, ploughing a bleeding furrow from ear to chin. The pores on her forehead weep the distillate of passion. She stares venomously at the back of the stranger, muttering.

'Gnawty childer . . . book gobbler . . . word eater . . . chews other bodies' words but won't make none himself . . . only whoochar, whoochar like a beastie.'

The stranger is hunched, abject beyond misery.

'Stupid, hairy, dumb flotsam. Is he pretty?' Vera demands. 'One pretty thing gottim . . . Flotsam's prettyful necklace, Gristy cross. Where's prettyness now? Beast lostit. Where? He don't know. He been too busy scratchim. Can't scratch hisself and keep him neckylace all in the one time. Too much workit. One pretty thing him lostit.'

The beast keeps his back to Vera but ventures a tentative arm behind him, insinuating his long, thin fingers towards her thigh. He looks around sheepishly then lowers his gaze. She scowls and slaps his hand. He hunches lower and whimpers softly.

'What does the beasty do?' Vera asks herself. 'Eatim foodies, all foodies and every foods, gobbles pratties. What Vera eat? Sand and rinds that beasty leaver . . . Praps he finds foods and brings some for Vera . . . Oh, no. Gobblebody only.'

The beast raises a gentle arm to softly smother her mouth. She swings her arm wide and fast to slap his ear. He slumps again and rocks gently, holding his hands to his ears to ward off further blows and words.

'Does the hairy body do any works? Just eatim, scratchim and walk around. Who cleanit house? . . . Vera.' She looks around her at the cave of the bush, 'Shittim hairy body, don't care for housey. Oh, no.'

The beast rises to his full height, shrieks, then flings himself on his belly, sinking his face in the sand and thrashing wildly with his legs. But Vera is not to be softened by mere agility.

'Well, Vera, even if beasty don't care for Vera at least he lookit after hisself, careit own body . . . Oh, no. Oh, no, he don't. He goim walkaround, gettim wet, gettim dirty . . . Seeim,' she is outraged, 'lostim crossy, whipples on his whopples, kelp in his earies, burrs in his furs, pissim bed.

'What is he? Growned childer. Oldy babby. Helpless, hopeless ninny body. Whatim use for? Nothing. Just Verachilder, Vera's babby.' She digs deeper with her nails into the weeping wound on her cheek. 'And whatem do to Vera's childer? Takem . . . Stealem . . . hittem little head with sharpy stoneys . . . makem hole in childer head, then buryem. Won't tell Vera the place. But Vera know . . . Vera watchem. She go and diggim out. But babby brokit. Won't move no more . . . cold and brokit like a hollow crabbit. When Vera love it, so them scrogglit.

'How Vera stoppem? Keepit childer sometime? Hideim? So what flotsam do? He goim walkabout. Show hisself to Hoggy, walkimround Parson, showim Folligaum . . .'

The anger is spent. The devils sated. Now she feels emptied, hollowed by melancholy. She dredges the words from the pit of her stomach and heaves them up, ordering their leaden weights on her tongue and, with exhausting effort, shoves them through the narrow gate of her numb lips, stuttering as strength fails her.

'Time goit. Spendit too fast. Wasteful beasty. They come takeim. Come useim. Allgone flotsam . . .

'Doctor lookim . . . Lordy come fuckim . . . Bailiff come

taxim . . . Hoggy skinnim furs . . . Parson damnim. Poor beasty, poor Vera. Always takeim.'

She sobs, but gently. The beast lays his hands upon her shoulders and strokes her, nuzzling her chill forehead.

'Alldone fixit . . . comem take beasty.'

The beast pulls her head on to his hot chest and rocks her, gazing down sadly at her matted scalp.

'Perish the gift,' moans Vera.

16
Ophal Mess

A figure burst from the merchant's house as if thrown. He landed on the balls of his feet, perfectly poised, then bounced forward. He had the stature and shape of Hogg, this man. In profile, he resembled a pear perched perilously on stalks – teasing gravity, which would have its revenge whatever the wait. The face was hidden by an impassive white mask on which were painted lurid red lips in a cupid's pout. His jacket was garish crimson. He skipped and whistled, then, as if stung on the rump by a hornet, shrieked and leapt, his whirling feet climbing the airs. As he proceeded on these ups and downs of his flutter-by path, he reached into his pocket, selected a coin and tossed it over his shoulder, hooting with raucous laughter. This couldn't be the merchant himself, for the figure jaunted unaided. He employed his very own legs.

Mistress Hogg and her betrothed daughter Cordelia watched the antics through the window of the attic room. Neither spoke for both understood. They had been locked in and had chosen to double the lock from the inside. Still, they turned skittery eyes to the door, as if sensing dangerous sounds from the other side.

This is a dangerous time. It is Ophal Mess.

'Since you will soon be a murridged woman, I must tell you your fate and the nature of men.' Mistress Hogg spoke with quiet sadness.

'Must I be coffled, mother?'

'A husband demands this. A wife grows accustomed.'

'Is it hurtful as it sounds?'

'At first it gives discomfort. With practice it awakes curiosity. Sometimes it causes amusement. But never laugh, daughter, for there lies danger. A man sheds his humour with his breeches and is stranger to the wit of his member. They are most proud of their part, be it wrinkled and limp as cod-liver sausage, or swollen and mad as rhubarb, sneezing like a rheumy nose. With patience one may learn to find pleasure around it as good as when pleasing oneself.' So Mistress Hogg cautioned her daughter in the trade of wifery.

The husband is the weather on the island of one's life. Sometimes it storms. It thunders and it flashes. It snows and it rains. It freezes then it warms. It pretends to shine but then turns cloudy. Else it threatens to storm but quickly clears. The weather is power – brute, blind, uncaring. Does the shepherd love the elements? He respects them. He bows to them. He knows they are fierce and changeable. He fears them. He gazes to the sky and predicts the passions. He does not complain. This would be foolish. He cannot instruct the sun.

When it warms, bathe in the sun. When it storms, seek shelter where the rains cannot reach you. Watch your husband's brow as the shepherd watches the sky. You grow accustomed and learn to read the clouds.

Each man is a different climate. Some scorch your earth. Some lash with rain. Some are kind and temperate. Each has his seasons. Adjust to them. Plant your corn in spring, harvest in summer, take shelter in winter. When it is autumn do not wish for the sun. What is, is.

The powerful are not wise. They have no need. Their life does not require it. That is woman's strength. She is forced upon her wits. The cleverest do not show their cleverness. Watch your husband but do not let him see you see him. Men believe themselves solid as stone, not empty as airs. Pretend you admire the granite as you look through the clear window of his person out on to the world beyond.

His body does not believe his mouth. But do not tell him so. This confusion is the wife's strength. You can read the signs and he cannot. He is the wind that blows itself along without knowing that it blows, nor even sees itself.

There is a conference of climates. Mad Vera watches from the doorway of her house and shakes her head. Men are converging on the beach. They approach from all directions. Some have passed close by. She has taken the precaution of disguising her home as a bush – removing the roof of sacking. She ducks inside at the sound of a crunching footfall.

A group has formed near the rocks. They pace around one another. Some shriek and splash in the pools left with the tide. These are not the sounds of sanity nor the acts of sensible men.

'Bad Ophal . . . Jahvy sleeps today. Time in a tangle.' Vera heaves anxiously, panting her words. 'Beastie stay abed. Men go crazed. Carnalval.'

There are only men. All have covered their faces with hoods or masks. Eyes twitch in their recesses, watching eyes sunk in their lairs. No man trusts another. Each flinches and jumps aside as another passes. It is as if they have gathered to fear each other. And still they swarm, faster and shriller.

The crowd forms a hollow, and a cassocked figure moves into its centre. All stop still. It is quite silent. The figure struts, leaning back to counterbalance the weight of a wooden phallus which curves out ahead of him, pointing his way.

He holds one hand cupped to an ear, as if to hear, while the other massages the member.

A second figure follows confused behind. He is dressed fine as a Lord, sporting a powdered wig. Pausing, bemused, he gazes uncertainly to his legs. Then, as if remembering the secrets of motion, the powers of legs, proceeds again.

The priest thrusts his phallacy back and forth as though coupling with the airs. Between his teeth he clenches a black and furry being. It shrieks pitifully, jerks frantically. The priest spits it out and catches it by the neck, holding it high for the crowd to see.

'Flesh of Ophal.'

He raises the squirming animal back to his mouth and crunches its rear quarters. The crackle of its bones carries through the air, like the snapping of twigs trodden on a path.

The Lord begins to pat his clothing, searching. He examines his pockets in turn, then chances upon his crutch. He unbuttons his breeches, encounters his member and pulls it forth, pissing into a bowl.

'Blood of Ophal.'

A man, padded to the shape of a Hoggy ball, is carried to the centre. He is held by four bearers, one to each spindly protruding limb. Lowered to the sand, he kneels for communion. The host is thrust into his mouth. His jaws are held tight as he gulps furiously for breath, then stretched wide open as the urine is poured cascading over his face. He is pushed forward, his face held in the sand, as the cassocked figure mounts him from behind. The priest thrusts in time to the chants of the crowd.

'Ophal . . . Ophal . . . Ophal.'

'Wicked peoples – naughty bodies.' Vera chides them softly from the door of her home. She pushes the beast back into the bush to prevent him learning any more.

17
Pork

'It's most improper.' Hogg was belligerent to his wife as though the fault were hers. Pips of blame squeaked through his perforated words. 'It is offensive to our good name.' He lied, of course. His was a friendless name, derided already, tainted by the pig for whose indecorous habits, gross appetites and carnal malpractices it should not have been held accountable. Yet, victim of resemblance, Hogg bore the shame whilst the culprit hogs scwaffled on uncaring. The merchant bristled and grunted as he suffered this new affront to a martyred name.

'Five days,' he snorted.

'Days . . .' his wife agreed, as was her habit. 'Five. All in a row.' Hogg scratched the peak of his belly through the woollen waistcoat. He kicked his footrest petulantly, scuffing the toes of his polished boots, wiping their reflections. His face was gorged with blood, crimson and growing darker. There was a purple tinge to his heavy jowls. His small pig eyes twitched and jumped, each to its different manic dance. At first he had been mild in limiting himself to anger. Then he had felt outraged to have been made the site of fury. Now he was convulsed with venom that he could not vent his spleen on its proper target. He yearned to castigate the stranger for his absence but could not do so. The stranger, conspiring shamelessly with logic, was elsewhere.

'No visit. No message, no gifts . . . no respect.'

'None of these and every other form of nothing.'

'Why, wife, does he do this?'

'There is no dumpling without a stew,' Mistress Hogg

observed piously. She brought the morality of the kitchen to bear on many issues in the confident assurance that her spouse would miss her points.

'What, wife?' Hogg snuffled and scowled.

'The hen can't stop the custards curdling.'

Things were indeed amiss. It was not clear if the cook, recipe or ingredients were to blame – perhaps it was the stove.

The best of murridges may be made from a virgin, a mature man of means and the flavouring of mutual advantage. It depends on the groom to thicken it. He must be frothed and fluffed with the airs of rhetoric. If the cook is less than careful, the mixture will not set. An excess of sugar may cause this. Cooking too fast yields a curdle.

Bake until set. To test for completion, slip the sharp blade of acquaintance into it. If it comes out clean and unsmeared the baking is done. The murridge may not be fully cooked in the centre, but there will be sufficient heat to the pudding to finish the bake.

The eggs had failed to thicken and bind the milk. The stranger had not come, as custom called him, to affirm his pledge with further gifts. Hogg had expected the token smile of some gold; the wink of cloths for the women's pleasure.

There was also the deficit of a haddock. The fish should have been sent, wrapped in oak leaves, that the wise augury of its tubes might pronounce upon the partnership. A dutiful father should seek guidance from the hues of the gills and the speckles of the belly. The portent of the liver is not to be disregarded, though its voice is less certain or clear.

'He seeks to slip the knot of our Trade, though he has sworn to Jahvy ... He compromises our daughter ... He cheats me ... I shall not allow this.'

'The pork is a wicked, resentful meat,' his wife agreed, 'its blood spoils quick and its guts fester early. You must roast it fast and fierce else it claims its revenge.'

A suspicion of his wife's meanings trod briefly in the mind of the merchant but was swept aside by the welter of his angers.

He should seek the counsel of the Parson and take with him some liquors for Lovegrave's communion. It was known that, when the spirits moved him, the Parson achieved sacred transports of the highest order — intense meditative trances, the exorcism of passing devils, the singing of tongues.

Murridge, Lovegrave reassured the merchant, does not require the consent of either party. Agreement is customary and often desirable, yet theology does not require it. The divine will does not await the say-so of frail man.

The precedents spoke clearly. The Deacon of Bevis, to remove the distant taint of bastardy, had married his grandparents though both had long ceased carnal coupling, being thirty years dead.

The Bishop of Broosk, it was known, frequented brothels for the salvation of souls. He would pass from room to room briskly murridging the squirming couples, converting their fornication to murrital duty, so snuffing the dangerous pleasures.

'Man must be confined,' the Parson poured a further beverage, smiling heavenward as the liquor descended his gullet. 'I say nothing of woman. Murridge is the proper prison for the lusts of man. It is a dark, severe place where passions perish. All should enter as they come of age and be held within. The bars are strong on the narrow windows, the chambers small and the walls confining. The gate is bolted by Jahvy and quite unyielding . . . I visit the inmates,' Lovegrave scowled most warmly, 'I act as stern warder. I tell them there is no escape. If left to their own devices, the convicts might take control of the jail, or conspire together to find some way out. With my firm guidance . . .' Lovegrave chuckled at his cleverness, 'they guard each other, sir. With but two to a cell they watch each other most closely. When one is wicked, the other tells the tale to me. It is better that man and woman confine each other, else they would wander the paths of sin to the horizon of Hull.'

'The Frenchman, sir?' Hogg reminded the Parson and

poured him more spirit. 'He forgets his promises. He plots an escape. He sneers at your offices.'

'Murridge is a sacrament, sir. As such it is beyond the consent of men. I murridge souls or I refuse. I tell them but I do not ask them. To seek the consent of men is to flatter them to know the truth. Worse, it invites them to judge the church, to pit their wills against the laws of Jahvy.

'Man does not agree or accept the sacraments, sir. He receives them or they are withheld from him. The baby does not ask for babtism. It resists. The devils within make it squeal and splutter. But we dunk it still that we may save it, lest it be spoke for Hull before it hears of Jahvy. The dying do not ask for unction. They ramble, oblivious of the judgement that shall damn them. The dead man never asks for his funeral, yet we pickle the body and say the words. From the brine he comes, to the salt he returns. I do not ask the degraded soul if she wishes for excommunication. I tell her – Vera – the church forgets you and reclaims your name. You are no person. We do not see you . . .' Lovegrave stopped and gazed vacantly before him.

'The Frenchman?' Hogg shouted at the Parson's ear but sustained his servile smile. Lovegrave jerked alert and began again.

'The sacraments steer man through the river of his miseries . . . Of women I say nothing . . . Life is but a blink in the eternity of the soul . . . but by that twitch are we all judged, finally and forever. The church tells man lest he judge for himself. Because I love men – even Frenchmen forsaking breeches – I will not let them choose. This man will honour his pledge, sir. Let his lusts be shackled by a wedlock for the welfare of his soul. If he evades us, we shall murridge him at a distance. But let us plot some means that he attend his wedding.'

18

The Murridge of Fur and Reason

Dawn had yet to break but the lights were bright in the merchant's house and the clatter of pots came loud from the kitchen, waking the birds, whose chorus began bewildered and shrill. All souls in the house were up, precocious from their beds, busied at their different duties.

Hogg was obsequious in service to his body, poised to bone and slice a smoked cod, having already met and mastered his barley gruel. His mistress wife had less ample frame, sparing her the heavier labours of eating. Some bread dunked in warm milk had sufficed. Now she stood at the kitchen table, despatching and summoning servants as a shepherd might whistle his dogs. 'Annie, the cheeses . . . Martyn, the baked eggs . . . Annie, the fresh breads.' On the table before her she collected, counted, ordered and recounted provisions for the day.

Alone in her room, Cordelia stood examining the solemn mystery of herself in the long mirror.

'Wife?' she mouthed silently, curling her tongue about the enigma, 'Wife?' But the meaning refused to bite at the bait of the word. She wore the clothes long gathered for this day – fawn linen dress sewn with ornamental dogfish teeth, lambskin shawl, pink ribbon in her hair. Her toes prickled, pinched by the tight leather slippers. She raised a hand to her breasts and shivered. In the mirror she could see nothing to reduce the strangeness or resolve the puzzle. A sullen face gazed back, bemused as she, yet detached and distant.

It was a solemn procession that left at first light. There was the panting of beasts and men of burden as hooves and feet dug crunching in the gravel path. Hogg was carried in front by his bearers. Though his lips twitched constantly, no sounds leaked out. Behind him, his wife rode the dappled mare, nodding to the rhythms of the beast's steps. Cordelia walked for she had no horse. Her eyes were cast down watching the tread of her sodden feet. Rivulets of brown water trickled from her reddened ankles. The hem of her dress was dirtied already, darkened by dew and speckled by grass seeds. At the rear of the group, muttering when spared the cough, Old Albert shuffled along, bowed under the yoke of the panniers.

They stopped at the doctor's cottage. Hogg leaned back in the sedan, patted his knee impatiently and closed his eyes for the wait. His wife watched the pulsing flanks of her horse. Cordelia stood in frozen stride, still gazing solemnly to her feet. Old Albert swore softly, dropped his baggage and trotted to the doctor's door which he kicked belligerently. It took several minutes and much battering for Gallimauf to peer out, bedworse and bleary, still befuddled by sleep.

'Fuff. Grist fut.' His parrot shrieked outrage from the depth of the cottage. 'Decent folk sleep.'

'Master Hoggy calls for you,' Old Albert explained grudgingly then turned his back on Gallimauf and proceeded slowly back to his panniers, satirizing the folly of haste by parodying the motions of running.

'This is the joyful day of our daughter's wedding,' Hogg spoke sullenly without turning to look at Gallimauf who paced alongside. 'First we collect the Parson, then we hunt the groom.'

The procession gained first in authority and then in popularity. Lovegrave now rode at the head, his aged donkey slowing their progress. Village folk gathered to the rear, joining at a proper distance as though coincidental fellow travellers on the same eccentric route. Daniel's boy scampered the length of the column, snaking in and out, grunting like a groom, then shrieking the news, 'Hoggy sell his daughter . . . Delia get her murridged . . . First catch the husiband.'

Though the party were three hours on the road, having toured the village twice, there was yet no sight or scent of the groom. Knowing his taste for elevation, all trees had been examined. Daniel's boy had climbed each on the route to scan its heights for hidden husbands.

They turned for the beach. It was thought the stranger sometimes paced the sands – though now he stalked the procession. As they pursued him, so he followed them, ambling along behind the hedge, peering out through breaks in the foliage, snorting with excited curiosity.

Hogg received in silence this news of the groom. His cheeks quivered and the veins of his neck pulsed urgently. Sweat broke from his furrowed brow. He was deep in the most tortuous and taxing of calculations without the companionship of pen or ledger. It involved the conversions of many currencies – pigs, pride, money, honey, honour, time and passion – at volatile rates of exchange. From the resulting figures it was necessary to subtract the price of integrity and the costs of appearances. Evidently he found an equation to his favour, for his forehead smoothed suddenly and the radiance of his goodwill shone through the open window of his face.

'Our son is most witty,' he conceded, 'our daughter is most fortunate.'

The wedding party gathered in the merchant's parlour. The crowd stood outside, some persons peering through the leaded windows. There was some hope that at this time of celebration some foods and wines might flow from the inside out, against the normal current.

The Reverend Lovegrave conducted the proceedings with tetchy haste. He spoke those tones of irritated instruction that he reserved exclusively for people. Missing from his voice were those modulations of enquiry that invite the participation of the couple.

'You do,' he told the groom. 'Be still, man. Take this

woman. Lend her the guidance of your will and body for the conduct of her life. And cease scratching.'

'Hucha?' Gallimauf whispered the question. The stranger merely shrugged and snuffled.

'He is uncertain,' the doctor explained, 'being torn between the celibate life of scholar and the guardianship of wife and childer.'

'And you,' the Parson glared at the bride, 'you are taken as wife by your master to serve him all your days.'

She released a quiet strangled sound, a comprise of 'aagh' and 'aye', perhaps.

'Then you are murridged. There is great joy.'

The groom's satisfaction with his new state was evident to all by his close attention to the ring. Its symbolism enraptured him. His knuckles had proved strangely narrow, none thick enough to retain the band. But he had toyed with it excitedly, tossing it from palm to palm, stowing it in a nostril then removing it to the privacy of an ear, then sucking it. All this showed the entirety of his commitment, whatever his earlier doubts. 'Murridge is the proper career of man.' This he spoke in mime – bowling the ring along the ground and following it chortling. The gesture was not wasted on his new parents. All prior doubts and misunderstanding were now resolved. Hogg and his wife beamed their proper and sensible pleasures.

This would be her last night at home and the last hour as sovereign of her body. Her mother had prepared the murridge bed. A bowl of fruits had been placed on the chest – a reminder of fecundity – lit then shaded as the single candle flickered to the breeze from the curtained window. The fleece had been drawn back on the bed revealing the stark white linen sheet. In the morning it would be hung blood-blotched from the window, confirming she had been properly pierced as wife. Cordelia let her shawl drop and shivered as she gazed to the line of her thighs beneath the dress. She drew the clothes over her head and laid them flat and tidy on the floor.

Stroking the silky slopes of her breast, she held a nipple

gently between finger and thumb. It raised itself, firm and warm to her touch. Her other hand ran down the curve of her belly to the curls of hair. Here and further. Within her. On her. Heaving, grasping, panting. She ventured a finger to the fold and pushed to enter an inquisitive finger. This could not explain it. She could not imagine.

He would know her as she could not know herself in revealing this, the adventure allowed to woman. What, then, would be the truth of it – pains, curious pleasures or laboured tedium?

He had feigned to ignore her after the vows, scampering boisterously, chattering, chortling, swilling wine. But when their eyes had met across the room he had paused momentarily, enveloping her in a brazen, promissory, lascivious leer. Then, she could not bear his eyes and looked away, reddening, her skin prickling strangely. His animal passion appalled her. Yet it also appealed. Now he would come to match his promises.

He was dangerous. A man without restraint who teased her father as none other dared: a man of careless wit and volatile humours, crafty and crazy as a fox. And now he would come to claim her, his dangerous energies focussed on her alone.

Would he find her adequate to his lusts? Were her legs too slender, her breasts too slight? Her passions too pale and insipid to his palate? Should she groan or whimper, or perhaps stay silent if this were a choice? What if the terrors seized her as he tore within? I shall not laugh, mother. You instructed me well.

She sat naked on the bed and shuddered. Still he did not come. The laughter below had grown hard and strained. Her father could be heard protesting. There was splintering of wood and the answering call of breaking crockery. The steps on the stairs suggested a scuffle. She blew out the candle and pulled the bedclothes tight over her head.

'No, sir, no.' Gallimauf's patience is strained, 'You have had wines enough, sir. You must attend your wife.'

Her husband chatters, aggrieved but docile. The door

swings open then immediately crashes shut, rocking the clothes chest.

'Lock it,' the merchant says, 'we have celebrated enough this murridge.' She hears the bolt being drawn on the outside of her door. The feet descend the stairs.

She hears the uneven panting of her husband. He paces back and forth at the end of the bed, rocking the loose boards which creak beneath his feet. His steps are the irregular paces of the drunkard. The bed judders and she feels the weight of his body on her legs. He lies there for some minutes, his breath growing regular. Her heart continues to batter her ribs.

'Chucha.'

'Husband?' Her voice surprises her. Though it does not tremble as she expects, it is weak and rasping.

He flings himself from the bed as though scalded, slipping on the polished timbers. She can hear his breath again, loud and uneven as though he were panting from exertion. He scampers around the room, tapping frenzied at the walls, colliding with the furniture, seeking a door and escape. There is a ripping of cloth as he tears the curtains down. She can see his outline now, hunched and heaving at the window.

'Husband?'

He shuffles over and kneels on the pillow by her head. She smells sour wine and some further pungency she could not name. Drips of fluid fall on her face like the most tentative of drizzles. He draws back the fleece that covers her and examines the slender length of her body. Turning her head from him, she draws her thighs together and holds her hands protectively to her groin. But he does not roll on her, or force apart her legs. He gazes merely and his breath grows quiet and calm.

Her body trembles, pale and opalescent in the moonlight. She withdraws her hands and splays her legs. He is neither fierce nor brutal, as she had feared, but strokes her belly with a gentle sliding finger and licks her shoulder.

'I am your wife. You are my husband.'

He lays his hand to rest on her belly, tickling her hip with a warm insistent tongue. Her hands hold his head tight to her body and she twists towards him.

'Beastie . . . beastie.' The voice is hoarse and plaintive and sounds from outside. He rises, grunting passionately, and shuffles to the window. Jumping upon the sill, he looks back hesitantly to his wife's bed. Leaping back into the room, he clutches the bowl of fruit to his chest, returns to the window and lowers himself nimbly from her sight.

Vera holds him tight to her bosom, then thrusts him away scolding, 'Naughtie beastie, stealing Hoggy's fruities.' But she takes the fruit, every piece, scooping them up and into her blouse. As they flee the garden, Vera tugging him by the arm, urging haste, they hear a desperate sound behind them. Cordelia breaks from her sobbing to the howl of a soul abandoned.

'Beastie, beastie, what you donnit?' Vera demands and hastens their pace.

19
A Sin Without Name

Others sleep.

Lovegrave's eyes pitch and roll to the storm of his dream. Froth bubbles at his lips, trickles to the chin and oozing over the precipice descends the cliff of his neck. His head twists towards his wife's foot. He clamps a toe between his lips and sucks ferociously. It is the most brazen of nipples rising from a voluptuous breast.

Lust moves the Parson though he is pledged to continence. To love a wife too ardently too often is to fall adulterer, to trespass for pleasure beyond the proper fence of murridge. Besides this night is triply proscribed. He has entered his wife already this moon: it is less than three days to communion, less than fifty days to Oaster.

They have taken the most stringent precautions lest the devil use their parts, moving them in sleep while the conscience slumbers. The Parson has strapped his wife's legs together, binding a belt around her knees else her thighs spread. She has laced him tight into his leather nightbreeches, bound his wrists, tying them by a thong to the head of the bed. They laid themselves down to suffer the night, head to toe, buttock to buttock, beneath the goat skins. The name of Jahvy had been the last word on their lips before sleep bore them to its bosom, thrusting a nipple into the Parson's mouth.

The breast is Cordelia's. She lies flat beneath him upon the altar, clenching and unclenching her fists, her belly quivering to the jerks of her hips, as she sucks him ever deeper within her. He spills in her and collapses moaning, but she continues to draw him with the shameless throb.

'You coffle my wife, then?' It is the Frenchman clothed in a cassock. He smiles benignly to the Parson, who is ashamed. He is naked. He has eaten of the tree and has known another man's wife.

'You seek salvation, sir?' The stranger is interested, conversational. Lovegrave rises to face him, holding his hands to his shameful privities.

'Salivation?'

'Man must be saved from sin. To be righteous he must first know wickedness. There is no merit to wanting nought, resisting nothing. As the condition of day is night, so good requires evil. They are the two faces of the coin – the head and the bum. Without lust there is no abstinence; without gluttony, no fast; without adultery, no fidelity . . . If man is to be saved from sin, he must first be sinner.' The stranger explained in patient tones, 'The greater the sin, the greater the salutation. Sin is the first, the greatest, the most difficult step on the path to salvation. It is a hard task and requires perseverance. But this is a pale and feeble sin, sir. Can you do no better? Man cannot find the highest path to salvation unless he treads the deepest chasm of sin. You are work-shy, sir. Jahvy does not stoop to save the dilettante.'

'There are worse sins?' the Parson is aggrieved.

'Seventeen. Yet one towers above the rest.'

'Swaffling a ewe? On Gristmas Eve?'

'Fut.' The Frenchman is derisive, 'That is but a fly at the arse of an ox.'

'More canino? With no clothes on?'

'But a single curly on Satan's privates.'

'Fluxolastry with one's other's mother?'

'Fuff. Nothing.' The stranger smiles unpleasantly, 'Should you sodomize seraphim on Sunday that would be nothing beside the sin.'

'Then I do not know it.'

'Then you cannot be truly saved,' the Frenchman declares,

with spiteful pleasure. 'That is the cruelty of Jahvy. He will not show man the highest path . . . It is the most original of sins and is without name. Men do not know it. Or, if they do, they do not know they know it. The pleasures of it are too rich and sharp to be matched to words. There are holes in the lexicon of ecstasy.

'This sin, sir, requires the yolks of two eggs, some vinegar and much oil. Though some say otherwise, mustard is unnecessary. The privates of a man are used as are certain parts of woman. The geometries of flesh are the secret of Satan whose numbers they express. The grammar of this curious coupling involves the strangest of combinations. It is unnatural, sir – there lies the pleasure and thus is the gate hidden. The curves are concealed and bizarre to the minds of man. It is so perverse as to make scrumbling with sharks seem natural as breath. Unless instructed a man may find this sin by the most curious of accidents. A rare man it is who chance upon it, and never more than once in his life.

'The pleasures of it are too powerful. They extinguish the flame of reason and wipe the slate on which memory's writ. So all who visit this sin, and practise its rites, immediately forget what they have done and the route they took to reach it. They are intoxicated and befuddled by this heaven on earth. Once descended from the heights of pleasure, they cannot remember where they have been or how to return. Their hair may be turned quite white. All they retain is a desperate sadness. They have known the garden then been cast out. Something is lost but they know not what it is. They stumble blindly from perversity to degradation, searching helplessly, but cannot recapture the lost sin. Nothing satisfies. The abomination of Onan is but a handshake, coupling a labour, yet they know not why . . .

'I can write you the prescription for this sin, sir, that you may visit it whenever you will – or, by resisting, find the highest road to Jahvy's kingdom.

'You will be sucked dry as an autumn leaf, left writhing and chattering like an imbecile. Your skin will be raw and bloody as a beetroot. Then, you will start again . . . The joys are exquisite, the thrusting thunderous, the tightness crushing. The suctions will draw your innards out. The squirming shames worms. The whimpering is deafening.'

'You seek my soul?' the Parson shrieks.

'I do,' the stranger concedes, 'though it is a small and sour thing, of little use to man or beast. But my master collects them, whatever their size or sweetness.'

'Flee, Satan, the wrath of Jahvy.' So shouting, Lovegrave kicks his wife from the murridge bed and wakes to the sounds of her wails.

20
Teeth

'I hired you as a two-handed man, Hooker. I was deliberate in that.'

'Yes, sire.'

'But now you hold your south-paw bandaged. It's swathed as a baby's nethers. Does it lie fallow in my service? Does one hand rest? Does the palm of the other claim pay for the both?'

The bailiff smouldered with grievance, all the time smiling like a bullied child to charm off further harm. How was he to convey the essence of this? Reality had failed to reveal the truth of itself, sneaking to hide behind the veil of appearances.

'I bleed for you, sire. I am wounded in your service – cruelly bit.'

Lord Iffe shrugged dismissively but spoke with a tinge of defence. 'I do not remember the exact occasion, but when I bite a man he does deserve it.'

'It was not you. It was the Frenchman.'

'Then you were careless. The French are notorious for their teeth.'

A bite has been just the bit of it. The bailiff had merely asked for the dues, and a farthing or so more, pressing the claim with a persuasive tug to the stranger's fur. In the face of this reason, the man proved rabid. First he bit, then he pulled hair, then he kicked to the belly. As Hooker hunched, winded, the man had seized his hands and swung him around, releasing him suddenly to fly an arc to the hedge. And he did not leave him to rest there, tangled in the briar, face in the mire. The Frenchman had jumped on his back. With the cool method of the assassin, he added considerable insult to no slight injury.

'How did you provoke him, Hooker?'

'I asked merely for the taxes due to you. He has bought himself a wife and owes you one quarter of the price. He has wandered Iffe using freely of the paths, stiles, trees and hedges, but has paid no tolls. He drinks your waters without recompense, inhales your airs without asking to rent them.'

'I will forgo the murridge tax for some nights with the bride. The other dues he must pay.'

'I told him of this convenience but he refused. He abused you in terms I cannot repeat.'

Iffe showed no curiosity.

'He called you a foul degenerate. He says you would infect his wife with many pox and several drips. He says you are ever poking your member where it never belongs.'

How did the man know of the spots? Was it within his powers to see through breeches? But the ills were not his. He was just brief host. They travelled around, these scabs and boils, and belonged to the commonwealth. And in their wake travelled Gallimauf with mercury poultice, chasing them off to other privates and charging each on the route. Anyway, Iffe had found his own remedy through proper metaphor. The pox was flee. Offer it a fresher, juicier perch and off it would hop.

'The spots have left me, Hooker. They have found another . . .' But Iffe trailed off, bogged in the mucous of memory. Some detail of this matter teased him but he could not sneeze it out. 'When you are fourteen and come of age,' his father used to promise him, 'you may bite your tutor and gob on the curate, but not vice versa and never before. At your age it would be improper.' So was that the truth of it? If none above Earl need bow to Chief Justice, if a Viscount might freely snub a Baron . . . given that even the youngest son of a Duke might cuff the ears of a yeoman . . . what rank of man might bite a bailiff?

'Have you told me the full of it, Hooker?'

The bailiff shuffled his feet, shame-faced.

'Well, man?'

'He pulled my hair, sire,' Hooker twisted his head to reveal the bald patch, 'and . . . he pissed on me, having thrown me down.'

'Pissed on you!' Iffe was delighted by this further detail. 'Then perhaps you have been privileged. To water you with such contempt, he must be a man of distinction.'

'He is a commoner. He has no rank.' The bailiff was adamant and disdainful. 'He comes of the merchant class, but he is radical. He speaks most ill of the aristocracy and particularly of you. His opinion, sire, is that you are a boil on the bum of the people. A bag of puss. He is surprised that no surgeon has excised you that the people might rest at ease.'

'Ease?' Iffe was outraged. Speech should not pass unpunished and, given the leakiness of his memory, it was often the last word he savaged most. When he pondered and sought the real culprit the whole collection would melt away. 'Thy people are not made for ease. Should they learn to dance, or play the harpsichord?'

'He asked me this question also,' Hooker said: 'When Adam delved and Eve span, who was then the gentleman?'

'It is a trick question, Hooker. Adam was the master but he was no gentleman, neither were his sons, as we know from the Book. But Jahvy saw the lack and was not too proud to improve the creation. He made the gentry later, then the aristocracy before he formed the angels.'

'What shall I do about the villain, sire?' the bailiff asked, dolefully holding his wounded hand to his chest.

'Summons him, on Sunday as is proper. You may surprise him in church. Sneak up behind when he kneels in prayer. And bite him if you wish. Your mouth is mine.'

21

Social Facts

Being the catalogue of villainies pursuant of Satanies –

These charges being writ by Gervase Gallimauf, Doctor of Words, Clerk of the Court of Iffe, also Physician learned in Biologics, also scholar being author of diverse long manuscripts including, not least, 'The Treatise on Human Nature' and 'Mathematics, Musics and Motions of the Spheres' – these being solely and exclusively his own mental labours and intellectual properties being in no part derived from or attentive to like-titled volumes by the scribbler known as Huyme or Muirpocks.

Whereas these charges are drawn up under the instructions of the Reverend Judge Ambrose Lovegrave – may he guard us from sin – under the jurisdiction of Lord Seymour Iffe of Iffe, they derive from the informations of several – Clovis Hogg, merchant and gentleman; Cordelia Hogg, woman, murridged of the accused; Theodore Hooker, bailiff and gentleman; Angus Brodie, labourer; Addis McGuigan, dead of the gripe, may he rest in peace. These evidences being further strengthened by the inductions of logic and supported by the truths of common knowledge and sound suppositions.

Let it be known that many wrongs, cheatings, heterodoxies, heresies, farragos, abominations and satanies have been committed by the Frenchman, resident of the Parish, who disdains to reveal his true name, being variously known as Doctor Sin, Devil, Beast, Huch, Shaggy, and clearly known and recognized by his surfeit of hairs, haunched posture and gross agilities. He being trader in clothes and beasts, also being scholar, though not known widely as author of any substantial manuscripts.

The wrongs being so numerous and diverse and grave it being facetious to order them of severity and beyond the hand of a scribe to list them all. Yet amongst his crimes this man, hereinafter the Frenchman, did this:

I. Murridged Cordelia Hogg, virgin of the Parish, and on his wedding night did violate her, *contra naturum, in amplexus reservatus,* reviling any conjugal debt, seeking venial pleasure, *non in debito vase.* In these crimes against Nature he did never think to the procreation of children nor to the proper employment of privities.

II. Having thus thrice ravished his wife did, that very night, abandon and desert her, with no provision for her support, so throwing her upon the alms of the Parish.

III. Did thereupon, even though it still be his wedding night, form an adulterous, lewd and licentious union, coupling rudely and unnaturally with no person, who has no name – before this being Elvira of the Parish – and who is known to consort with diverse devils.

IV. Did despatch devils of his acquaintance upon gentlefolk and other persons of the Parish causing grievous sicknesses, argumentations and other ills, these including the deformation of calves, the souring of milks and the scouring of pigs.

V. Amongst these devils being Incubi and Succubi which visited gentlefolk without respect of their position and continence and coupled with them shamelessly, *indebitus modus,* causing great torments and suffering, these pains being magnified by it being a holy season and a solemn fast.

VI. Whereas he did agree a bride price with the vendor, Clovis, having sworn this, did not thereinafter pay due monies or beasts, nor interest on non-payment, nor has the intentions to do so. Thus has he stolen a wife.

VII. Likewise he did refuse payment of the due taxes to the Lord Iffe for privilege or murridge or for sojourn and movement on Iffe.

VIII. In refusing so, he did with teeth, feet and hands, sorely assault the person of the bailiff.

IX. This being an assault on the person of the Lord Iffe himself; the bailiff being his servant, voice and arms.

X. He did foment insurrection, committing much violence with mischievous and malicious mouth against the Lord Iffe.

XI. This being an assault upon Jahvy himself; the Lord Iffe being his servant, representative, voice and ears.

XII. He did preach degeneracy, wickedness and sins and did variously contest and reject the natural order.

XIII. Especially, he did seek to promote by example malpractices of nakedness that he might encourage concupiscence and venereal excess.

XIV. By payment of gold he did bid to buy the souls of Angus Brodie and Addis McGuigan, which offer these good men did fiercely resist by pleading that Jahvy might save them, which he did, praise be the Lord.

XV. Did argue the compound heresy –
    i. That creator of the universe is not Jahvy but the other god who is Lucifer descended.
    ii. That angels couple, so reproducing themselves in sin.
    iii. That the organs of generation are the site of the soul.
    iv. That in venereal sin do souls mix and know each other.

v. That man should perch in trees and disdain the earth.

vi. That the world is the shape of a bubble and that man is enclosed on the inside, so gazing to the centre.

XVI. Though it be the least of his sins, that this man was ever the hypocrite. Whereas the man did smilingly take of all hospitalities and guidance from the gentlefolk of Iffe who mistaked themselves as friends, he did ever sneer and abuse them when their backs were turned. In return for the loan of a book, this man did shamelessly eat the fifth part of his patron's library, spitting the words to the wind.

The Frenchman is called to trial to answer these charges, as best he may, offering the surety of his skin.

22

The Profession of Monkey

Dampened by drizzle, Vera and the beast have risen early from their fitful sleep and sit on the sands at the doorway of their bush. They lean shoulder to shoulder and watch out through the swaying grasses to the misty curtain hanging heavy above the waters.

Vera knows melancholy. Asleep the terrors visited her. She pleaded first, then screamed, that they should free her beastie. Awake, she is held by a weary sadness that makes her strangely gentle. She has ceased to scold the beast, as though resigned to his whims and ways. The apple she passed him is returned as core, pressed firm and wet into her palm, but she does not complain. She is distracted, sniffing the air. Her brow folds to announce suspicions.

There is a presence asea, a dark grey shape, rolling gently on the mist, menacing by its vagueness. This excites the beast. His nostrils quiver. He crouches to watch the shape and turns an ear to the wind to catch the distant creaking. The hairs rise on his neck and scalp. He stands to his full height and swings his arms.

'Do you know it, flotsam?'

He ignores her. He is alert to this presence and knows nothing else. Vera reaches up to hold his wrists but he pushes her hand away and launches himself down the dunes. He chatters and chortles as he romps along the beach. At the frothing line of the shore, he leaps and somersaults, waves and shrieks.

* * *

The ship lowers a boat, scraping and jerking down its side till it meets the bounce of the waves. Four men row, dipping and pulling to grunted commands. A figure in scarlet stands at the stern. In the bow there is a huddle of three hunched men. At an even distance between ship and shore, the boat rests to the will of the water. The oars are raised high then lowered, like the folding limbs of a beetle. Two men in the bow rise, then slip over the side. The third can be heard protesting. He is surrounded and held, the boat pitching wildly, then thrown to the waves. Whilst the other two swim slowly and purposefully to the shore, his head rises and falls in a thresh of white water. His hands stretch high, clawing for leverage on air. The sailors watch silent till the soul finds rest. Then the oars are returned to the water and swing the skiff back towards the mother ship.

The beast shrieks his pleasure. His voice rises the scales of excitement as the swimmers draw slowly towards the beach. Alerted by his chatter, they tread water, their bobbing heads watching him. They strike out again, but at an angle so they may land further along. The beast scampers down the beach, anticipating their landing point. They pause again watching his frenzied gymnastics. They have formed a plan for they swim apart now, to the right and left of him. The beast sways from side to side but cannot choose. Tortured by indecision he howls his protest, jerking his head from side to side as the two men wade through the shallows up to the sands.

The twins smiled to one another, but the gesture carried a taint as if spoken from a furtive code, saying more and less than friendship. They had been surrounded and led firmly by the arm to the inn. Now, with beers in their bellies, and more being plied upon them by the dull, fat man with the pig eyes, they smiled sly pleasures.

It was a cold, grey and desolate place but worse could be expected of prisons. The walls were the waves and each man his own warder. Also, there were women.

'We did not think to find ale here.' Matty drained his mug sadly to the dregs.

'We feared there would be no ale,' Hatty agreed solemnly. Hooker refilled their mugs.

'It is not allowed to sup ale on the Lord's day,' said Hogg, 'nor on holy fasts. But provided a man be moderate, as long as he finds no pleasure in the beverage, there is little harm.'

'There must be rules,' Matty observed piously.

'Indeed. We are hospitable to those who follow the laws of Jahvy,' said Hooker, 'but not all strangers understand this.'

'To the Lord Jarvie,' said the twins, 'who leads us here and guards us well. His will be done.' They clinked their mugs together.

'You are most similar to the eye,' Hogg looked studiously from one to the other and back again, 'and quite equal to the ear.'

'Others have thought this and told us so,' Matty said. 'We are kin and both borrow from the family face. This is my brother whereas I am myself.'

'And you are slight in the upright.'

'Alas, that is our stature. Before we grew we were even shorter.'

'There is another . . . short like you.' Hogg spoke with great care, watching both brothers and how they watched each other. 'Perhaps you know him.'

'Sir?'

'He is short, much hairy and chatters.'

'The monkey? He greeted us. He met us when we came.'

'Money key?' Hogg asked.

'Monkey . . . Mon-key,' the twins sniggered unpleasantly at the yokel.

'Yes,' said Hogg, 'he is my daughter's husband. But we do not know him as monkey or name him so. What profession is monkey, what rank of man?'

'Well now . . .' Hatty looked earnestly to his ale, 'to be a monkey is a queer career. It is a hereditary title like that of king. One is born to it and so elect. Others may imitate and ape the features but we know they are mere pretenders . . . To be monkey, sir, is most demanding. It requires the breeding of a prince, the fairness of a judge, the intelligence of a merchant, the morality of a bishop and the energies of many children.'

'Yes,' Hogg was impatient, 'but what does monkey do?'

'Often he chatters, scratches himself and eats fruits. Climbing is most dear to him. He is very agile . . . When he is bored he plays with his parts.'

'All this is true,' said Hogg, 'but it is known to every man. What I ask is the profession of monkey. What works does he do? How does he make his monies?'

'Work? Work, sir?' Matty chuckled, 'But he does not work. In that he is like a Lord. He does not work or feed himself but lives on the labours of others. He is an example to us all. Like our king, his task is decorative . . . You must be proud, sir, that your daughter has wed into the monkey class and ennobled your line with his breeding.'

Hogg and Hooker withdrew to a corner and conferred, whispering furiously and gesturing with the frenzy of monkeys.

'We shall take you to secure lodgings,' said Hooker to the twins. 'You will not be disturbed till we come to talk to you more.'

Matty looked to his brother, who nodded. They should advantage themselves of the full width and depth of this hospitable place.

'If it is no trouble to you, sirs, we would ask for one comfort more. We would much enjoy a woman, being several days without. As brothers, we are not too proud to share.'

23
The Doctor's Defence

A buttress of light reached from the floor of the cell to the single, small barred window high in the wall. The airs in this golden shaft were clouded milky by dust. Over the aromatic sweetness of hay there was the acrid bite of the uncleaned stable.

Gallimauf heard the rattle of chains and an angry chattering, but through the dusty haze he could see nothing of the walls of the cell which were built from blocks of blackness.

The beast advanced into the light to the full length of his tether, tugging at the chain as if to tear it from the wall. He spat, bit upon air and fixed the visitor with fanatical eyes. The light formed a halo of the erect hairs of his head.

'Are you well, sir? I thought I would call on you and enquire of your health.' Gallimauf spoke with casual amiability though he could tell that the man was angry. As to his health, it seemed that he had suffered from five days of imprisonment. His fur was matted and had lost its lustre. His eyes had wept a yellow mucous which clung to his lower lashes. Across his back were blood blisters and livid stripes where the persuasions of the rod had been tested but found wanting. Despite three savage beatings he had remained obdurate. He had refused to confess. He would not implicate his accomplices.

The doctor reddened and looked away. The beast sustained his ferocious gaze.

'You will not shame me, for I have done you no wrong.' The doctor was adamant, but the prisoner rattled angrily, jerking at his chain.

'There can be no question of any betrayal. In the matter of writing the charges, I merely did my duties. It is my task. I am Clerk to the Court. I must write the account. Those accusations were never mine but sprang malicious from the mouths of others. My task is to scribble, not agree or dissent. But if you wish my candid verdict, sir, the charges are excessive. You are no satanist, no devil.'

Wearied by the futile struggle to reach Gallimauf, the prisoner turned his back and, clanking his chains, retired to the dark cave of his corner.

'Tell me, sir,' Gallimauf diplomatically changed the subject, 'before you ate the *Treatise*, did you consider Muirpocks' discourse that there can be no knowledge outside of discourse? Did you note the flaw? If all is relative to our language, so is relativity itself.'

Sullen and distracted, self-pitying perhaps, the prisoner had no mind for philosophy.

'I have brought you an apple.' The doctor withdrew the fruit from his jacket pocket and bowled it along the ground into the dark corner. 'My friend, I thought, would enjoy an apple. I have polished it for you. It is most clean and quite unblemished.'

The apple returned instantly from the dark place it had visited, striking Gallimauf hard between the eyes. He wiped the pulp from his brow and rubbed hard against the pain.

'You are not perfectly couth, sir. You are ingrate.' Might the man still bear a grudge at the way he had been captured? 'I guess your grievance but it is misdirected at me. You believe I tricked you, embracing you, then leading you here. But that was for your sake, sir. The men with me wished to seize you and break some bones as they did so.' The doctor paused and allowed time for this sense to register on the beast. 'So you see, I ever acted to spare your blood. I worked for your interests.'

Gallimauf approached the prisoner cautiously, extending a tentative hand. The man spat at him and hunched as if to lunge. The doctor retreated hastily beyond the reach of the chain from the radius of malice.

'I can conjecture why you are angry still, despite my accounting of my clean conduct. It is the matter of the beatings, is it not, sir?'

The prisoner chattered nastily, his spiteful innuendo harsh and unjust on the doctor's ears.

'It is because I asked the questions as they beat you?' Gallimauf laughed uneasily at the faux pas. 'If that is the problem tell me. It is easy to explain.' But the man neither spoke nor stirred. 'This was to spare you, lest they find some harsher interrogator. And did you notice how I spoke coldly to you? That was to conceal our bond, so that they might trust me fully . . . And all you had to do was speak – to plead your sorrow. If you had said the words, I would have bid them stop. But no, you would not answer me. You denied me thrice, then more . . .' Gallimauf shook his head, self-righteously perplexed, 'And do you remember? I bid them spare your head and limbs and limit their strokes to your back. And what good has your silence done you, sir? You are scrutable. Your accomplices have told on you. They have disclosed the ways of the monkey class.'

The Frenchman whimpered as he heard this news. Twisting both hands behind his back, he ran his fingers gently across the wounds.

'But I remain your friend, sir, your only ally. I shall speak in your defence. I have a radical and ingenious account of your conduct . . . There is some cost. If you shed the hand that stole, donate your tongue that lied, settle your debts and ask clemency . . . they will let you live. Listen carefully. The defence lies this way . . .'

It is a simple truth, the doctor explained, yet easily forgotten. We are each at war with ourselves. There are battling forces within a single head.

We may rise, put on our trousers, then immediately take them off and retire again to bed. Then we rise again, but are distracted from our trousers by the conversations of our parrots. We might pour water in our mother, then bid 'good morning' to our kettle. This much is common sense, but there is a further twist.

The several of ourselves, forever disagreeing, are ever changing – and what we were is gone. A man is different from the person he was yesterday, because he has experienced and learned. And tomorrow's soul is different again, informed as he is by today.

And yet there is a perversity at the root of what men term justice. The effect is held responsible for the cause.

Today's self, chastened and sorrowful, is punished for yesterday's self who did the dirty deed. And what is the sense of that? Is the man responsible for the child he grew from? Is the chicken accountable for the egg it was? Should we praise the bacon for the pig? Blame the puddle for the puppy, censure the wreck for the storm?

We live and often learn, but are condemned from our perch of wisdom for the errors we once made. They who judge flee the present to reside in the past. They assess you by what you were and never what you are. They are so concerned with catching up with yesterday that they cannot imagine today, or even remember tomorrow.

'It is a compelling truth, sir?' Gallimauf beamed his triumph. 'Sever yourself from sin. Disown the self you were. Cease your monkey ways. Show your contrition and be born again.'

24

Trial and Metamorphosis

If they fear the Parson Lovegrave it is not solely for whom and of what he speaks. It is for the awesome power of his words. With the merest twitch of his lips, in the deceptive ease of his tongue, betraying no passion beyond a mild contempt, he achieves the most mysterious alchemies. Infants gain names, the hasp of man and the clasp of woman are forged into a wedlock, Morphy's biscuit is made the flesh of Grist, devils are driven out, sinners briefly regain the lost flavours of innocence. So it was that this work day became holy day and the long barn was rechristened as court house. He just said the words and dripped the water – itself but pond-water till charged by sounds to holy juice – and the house of the beasts became palace of law. He said it was court, it was court and everyone saw the truth of this. There lingered, though, signs of the transubstantiation. A pungent steam rose through the bed of straw from the rotting stew of dung below. A nanny goat remained, tethered to an iron hoop in the wall. As she nursed her kid, squeaking and thrusting at her udder, she eyed the people with peevish belligerence, in ignorance of law, as if this place were hers.

A trestle table had been placed at one end of the barn. Sitting in stout oak chairs behind it were the Judges Lovegrave and Hooker who spoke in turn for the powers sacred and profane. Both were wigged. Lovegrave's wig rode high, bobbing on his ginger mane. Hooker's was loose, encasing his head like a helmet, its silver curls lending him the appearance and dignity of a sheep. They exchanged wigs but the effects persisted, for both hair-pieces were the same size, being loaned by the Lord Iffe whose single head was moderately proportioned, being neither too small nor large but very much ideal.

Some six paces from the judges' bench a post had been sunk deep into the boggy ground. The Frenchman, his arms knotted tight behind him, had been bound to the wooden stake. He had been gagged. It was yet to be decided whether he could speak. There were contradictory issues of the greatest moral import. A man has a right to defend his life with his tongue – to speak his account, state his sorrow, concede his guilt and plead some clemency.

But the privilege of the person should not be paid from the purse of the commonwealth. It was feared that the man might abuse his right, launching some invectives, savaging with the sinister wits of his tongue those who are defenceless, defying the just processes of law, denying the truths of Jahvy, making parody of his accusers and mockery of his trial. It would be a travesty should he clamber from the abyss of guilt to the elevation of a pulpit from which to preach perversity.

Gallimauf sat to the side of the prisoner at a small desk. He was in sober black as befits a clerk. A broad, heavy ledger lay before him and he gazed excitedly at its pristine pages. He had ravished several geese for their strongest wing feathers which now lay as sharpened quills in a row by his book. He would show the speed and elegance of his calligraphy. He would write most fast without moving his lips. Those who watched would wonder.

Behind him, filling the space of the barn, were the people. All were summoned to follow on from church. As modest humble folk who obliged their lords and obeyed the words, they were strangers to the rites of justice. They stood hushed and cowed by the enormity of a trial.

Clovis Hogg – merchant, husband, father, victim – was borne piggy back to face the bench as witness. Old Albert knelt so that his master could sit easy on his shoulders and rest his feet on the ground. The merchant's sorry tune was ornamented by the continuo of Old Albert's panting wheeze.

A father's duty is a terrible load. He cherishes a daughter

and devotes his life to her cause. Then he must allow her to follow her whim and give her love to a husband. A father must bear this loss without show of pain. He may interfere only to ensure that the suitor is an honourable man.

Here lies the crux. What a man does not know, he cannot imagine. If he is honest, he believes others so. Because he is candid, he trusts to the appearances of others. As he trembles before Jahvy, he assumes reverence in others. He loves his daughter with such an ardour, he cannot imagine another might feel her different.

Yet all in the Frenchman was abuse and deceit. When this man spoke of virtue it was like a mole extolling the heavens. His sinister plans were greased by the honour of his trusting victim. He borrowed monies without repaying them on the surety of his vulgar wealth. Pretending the manners of a prince, the sanctity of a monk, he stole a wife and ravished her horribly. Hogg wept, rocking on the unsteady chair of his servant's shoulders. Smearing the tears on his crimson, bloated face, he pointed a moist limp hand to the prisoner, 'He has robbed me of honour, money, daughter and peace . . . He has brought me down.'

Such was the gravity of Hogg's sorrow, the weight of his shame, it required the aid of a further bearer to carry him back to his place in the court.

Judge Hooker rose and walked from the bench to the place of witness. He doffed his wig and swore solemnly his truth and virtue. He told of many crimes of the prisoner – of taxes refused, bites given, respect withheld, subversions spoken. He told indirectly of worse sins too gross to be spoken baldly.

Matty and Hatty were led limping in to the court and stood head bowed before the judges. Though both had both eyes blackened it was now easy to tell them apart. One had had the right ear docked whilst the other had surrendered his left.

'Tell me, leftie, do you know the prisoner?'

'He is monkey, sir.' Matty spoke dully and wearily through swollen lips as though reciting the catechism.

'What are monkeys?' asked Hooker.

'They are desperate, debauched . . .' Matty fell silent and rolled his eyes, struggling to remember.

'They are desperate, debauched, depraved degenerates?' asked Hooker.

'Exactly so, sir.' Matty gave the judge a thin smile of gratitude, 'They are very naughty, sir.'

'What do you know of monkeys?' asked Hooker. 'I speak now to the right ear.'

'They behave like beasts. They aren't to be trusted except by other monkeys and then but rarely. There is little honour amongst monkeys. Though they seem friendly enough, they suddenly turn wild, biting, punching and kicking. They are most deceitful in this, smiling when angry.'

'Are monkeys honest in Trade?' asked Judge Hooker, though he guessed the truth already.

'Indeed not, sir. They are the most unscrupulous of men. Though they borrow on promises, they never repay. But above borrowing they prefer even to steal. By this plan they aim to gather to themselves all the wealth of the world. They are so infamous across the waters that many will not trade with them even the time of day.'

'What are the carnal practices of monkeys?'

'They are the rudest and lewdest of people. They do things that a modest man cannot even name. Often they throw off their clothes that they may couple at a moment's whim. They do this sometimes without even asking the partner's name. Though they spawn many children, they shun wedlock. It is a rule amongst them that each be a bastard. They are proud of this.'

'How does the church regard the monkey class?'

'As satanists, sir. Across the water, no church will admit them . . . will not babtize, nor christen, nor bury. The rites are held from them for monkeys conspire with the devil. It is said by many that it was monkeys disguised who nailed Our Lord.'

'Monkeys are always radicals who usurp their lords?'

'They are, sir. They despise all lords without exception.

They plot the overthrow of princes that they may rule in their stead. The monkeys of all nations combine in this aim.'

'Then it seems,' said Hooker, 'that monkeys are the wildest of men who threaten all laws, morals and order.'

'Indeed, sir. This is well known.'

'And how is this one compared to others of his kind?'

'In all my life and travels, I have not heard whisper of a more wicked one. He is the worst of the worst.'

'Does the right ear agree in this?'

'It is just so, my lord. I am ashamed to be near him.' Hatty smiled, his duty completed.

'And you?' Hooker asked, his tone now curdled and sour, 'You and your brother are his partners?'

The brothers looked at each other, their bruised faces contorted by fear and shocked by this treachery.

'No, no, no, sir . . . No . . . We do not know him.'

'You are his accomplices,' Lovegrave said, severely and decisively. 'Though you seek to deny it, it is clear that you are monkeys also and play your part in the monkey business. He is the master. You are the lesser monkeys. You have betrayed yourselves. You know his plans too well . . . You shall not escape by betraying your master.'

25
Discipline and Punish

The bailiff led in the delegation. The men stopped at the fringe of the carpet and watched the back of their lord who continued thrusting, coupling with his harpsichord, oblivious of their presence. Iffe's head jerked on its stalk, his back quivered as his forearms pumped the prancing fingers. His legs were in spasm beneath the machine. The audience stood transfixed by this carnal congress. There was such passion here, requited in intensest pleasure, that they knew they witnessed some serious sin.

It was no proper melodic tune like 'The porpoise loved his herring wife', nor solemn humn such as 'Jahvy leads us by the nose', but was rather a crazed cascade. It was beyond the means of a mouth to whistle it, being too greedy and garbled of sound. As soon as you noted a tune, another would nudge it aside or tease it cruelly. When you tapped your right foot the left would immediately commence a different patter, your cheeks would twitch, your head nod, and you'd be off in a Vitus dance.

Iffe concluded on a crashing chord and slumped panting over the keyboard, jerking in spasm. Gallimauf coughed twice to alert the master to spare him further shame. Iffe raised himself from the bare chest of the instrument and turned glazed eyes on his visitors. He gazed bemused for some moments then waved them off, 'Go. The recital is over. Bach is finished and I am spent. I cannot come again.'

'We have disturbed you on a matter of justice,' said Hooker. 'We have tried a man and found him guilty. He has done the worst and then much more.'

'Thrash him,' Iffe said wearily. 'Continue until you finish, then beat him some more.' He flicked a limp hand dismissively in the direction of the door.

'A thrashing is too mild and kind. We wish to erase the blot of his ugly life. We need your permission for this.'

'A snuffing?' Lord Iffe revived, his eyes focussing bright and sharp. 'A snuffing isn't nothing. This demands some scrutiny. It would be a lesson to the people and must be well taught. What has he done?'

'Lewdness,' said Lovegrave. 'Concupiscence, sacrilege, bestiality, heresy, robbery, satany, provoking riots, consorting with devils, deflowering virgins, all three forms of adultery after several forms of fornication, conspiring . . .'

'Treason, importuning, being a suspicious person,' Bailiff Hooker took up the baton, 'he bites, shows disrespect, assaults bailiffs, bites parsons, impersonates, goes naked, commits satire, screams suggestiveness, refuses taxes, acts the braggart, eats salaciously, consorts in a vain manner, subverts, cheats, is contemptuous.'

'Purloining, pilfering, spoliating, abstraction and subtraction, diddling, swindling and defaulting,' Hogg spoke with controlled fury, 'and dissembling, evading, deception and abuse of trust. All these without mentioning the rudeness and fraudulence of his manners.'

The others turned to Gallimauf, who looked shame-faced to his shoes, then reluctantly complied. 'He ate the best portion of my library. He taught nonsense to my parrot . . . He has declared war on reason. He is an epistemological anarchist.'

'He has been most thorough and energetic,' said Iffe, 'but were there sins he left untouched?'

'He has not made any graven images,' Gallimauf conceded fairly, scrupulous as ever, 'or none that we know of. He has not coveted another's beasts. He has killed no kings.'

'That cannot be enough to save him. How do you think to spend him?'

'There are a wealth of alternatives,' said Gallimauf and counted his fingers briskly. He had been waiting this moment and had prepared his speech. Later he might write down the ideas. This would be 'A prolegomena to a discourse on the symbolisms of various modes of arresting human motions'.

'. . . each alternative has its virtue and each its unfortunate face. Every form of execution carries a special message in speaking more than a death.

'Stoning is engaging. All may join in with a vigour to match their outrage. But this carries the taint of democracy, making the people the agents of law.

'Hanging is humane and so we must consider it. However, it is limp of metaphor – a brief, suspended, strangled gesture.

'Decapitation is startling, so quick, so sure. It is philosophical too. It speaks the dualism of mind and body. The soul – which we know lies above the neck, perching in the pineal body – is freed by the hatchet from its bodily house. It may linger briefly, contorting the face, swivelling the eyes, twitching the lips to say goodbye. Glazed on the eyeballs of the disembodied head are the last sights of the departed soul.

'Burning or boiling prepares the soul for the afterlife. It is instructive, a discouraging example for those who remain. It is very disagreeable to baste oneself in one's very own oils. There is much distress for those who witness. The eyes weep, the ears crackle and the nose revolts. Those who have watched a witch burn will not eat for several hours and cannot stomach roast meats for many days.'

'Fuff.' Hogg stared contemptuously at Gallimauf, forcing him from the path of hyperbole to the verge of silence. 'I want his furs,' said Hogg. 'He owes me still. He may settle his account with his skin. I will lay it on my lap when the evenings are cold. I will think of him then.' The merchant stared at the wall, ignoring all eyes. He had decided.

'What of his family?' said Iffe. 'They will claim the body which is rightly theirs.'

'I am his family, his closest kin,' Hogg gave a tight smile. 'His is my daughter's husband.'

'Then there is no difficulty. When he is gone you may make

a purse of his ear should you wish. You might retain whichever parts you choose to remember him by.'

'When I say I want his furs,' the merchant explained, 'I want him to know he gives them.'

'Then tell him so before he leaves us.'

'You do not understand.' Hogg resumed his exasperated tone as though explaining a simple truth to a stupid child, 'I wish him to give his furs whilst he is with us still. As his furs are rolled from his body, I wish him to think – "I give my furs to Hoggy whose daughter I married" – Thus he can repay me as his final act in life.'

'It is elegant,' Gallimauf nodded excitedly. 'It is most proper. This is how Mani died, the most infamous of heretics . . . In this mode we might mark his heresy for all to see, yet allow him to settle his debts and clean his slate . . .'

There was something else that the scholar wished to say. He bit his lip then held his mouth open but mute.

'Yes, doctor?'

'It is this . . . the man might further help us by contributing to our science. If the merchant has the fur, sir, I might claim what lies beneath. I am engaged in a treatise. The flesh would be most useful. I research how the psyche is betrayed by the soma, the soul described by the body. The Frenchman is most curious, peculiar both of mind and body. I should write the account around him. If Hoggy would lend me the flesh, I should give him a footnote of thanks. I would return his relation promptly as soon as I had charted him . . . I should pickle him at my own expense thus saving the family the cost.'

'Enough of this flesh trade.' Lord Iffe snapped his impatience, 'I shall see the man. I shall decide.'

The Frenchman's arms were bound behind him. From his wrists hung a leash that joined him to the warder. The man prodded him forward on the business end of a rusted spike. The prisoner ignored all except for Gallimauf at whom he hissed and spat.

'Tie him to the chair, then leave us be.'

Their last sight was of Iffe circling the prisoner and

chuckling softly. It was a long and muffled interrogation. When Iffe appeared again it was not to speak his decision but instead to summon provisions. 'Apples,' he shouted, 'she is frightful fond of fruits.' He retired again with the food, a man brisk with purpose. All that could be heard, and only in intimate proximity to the door, was the quiet grunting of the prisoner, as though he were in sober agreement with the Lord Iffe's observations. Then the prisoner fell mute and Iffe it was who took over the task of grunting. After a long passage of silence there was a bout of laughing, some squealing – both singular and plural – and the scraping of furniture dragged over the wooden boards. One of the two had hiccups before quiet ruled again.

When Iffe finally pushed open the double doors he seemed curiously dishevelled. His shirt was creased and hung loose outside his breeches. There was a moist pinkness to his forehead as though he had attempted exercise.

The prisoner lay untrussed, sprawling, legs splayed upon the carpet on a bed of apple pulp. He heaved drowsily and snuffled. He wore the expression of a drugged or drunken man.

'She is a simple soul and harmless,' Iffe smiled down at the Frenchman. 'Though she is not handsome, she is most affectionate and kind.'

'He is a monkey,' Hooker protested.

'Indeed . . . She is my first monkey.'

'May we have this body now, sir?'

'Take her then,' Iffe yawned wide. 'She will allow you whatever you wish, so long as you first please her with some apples and some rum.'

26
Chatterhowl

Whenit?

Jahvy day to make it holy. Takem beastie horrigible just like Vera knewit.

Howit?

Rippim, skinim, beastie screamim, chatterhowl, twitchim. Spillem beastie juices. Pinkan yellowim, shakim, squealy poor flotsam. Cry like cut piggy till soul go flitterout.

Hangem both badbody runties. No hurt. Just jerk then deadem . . . but pealem beasty coat. Howlim, laughem . . . dicem beasty belt. Rollem bloody body, pullim legs, breakem beasty teeth, smashem pretty pearlies, smearem reddit. Shriekem.

Jahvy watchem. Vera can't lookit. Vera can't leavim . . .

Jahvyworkit . . . hollowholy . . . peabody godit. Grokelrattle.

Ribmeat vommitim. Veracussim. Vera kisser devils. Gristcrap.

Whyem?

Whatim donnit poor flotsam? . . . stealim fruities, eatim small story, climbim hoggy hole, stealit hat. Nuthin baddim. Only silly body. All childerplay . . . But Gullyfoam speakim, Hoggy thinkim, Iffy fuffitall for beasty blamit.

Whatem are, givit beasty. Festerguts and dungheads. Vomitout insides for smearem beasty skin. Killemselves in beasty body. Makes flotsam screamem.

Cosim Vera's. Always havem Vera's. Always breakit. Vera promise Vera, Vera payem.

Persons hates peoples. Smearem weakies, eatem runties, suckem marrow, scrunchem bones.

Suffrem childers. Whiffem hole and stuffit. Smellem free to sellit. Sniffem life so snuffit ... seeit run, breakit leggies. Hearit laugh and squashit. Watchit fly to cage it. Born it, so pickle it. Breathe it so chockit neck. Seeit see so pokit eyes out.

27
Lamb

Though they do not like each other, they do not feel dislike. Theirs is a bond beyond friendship, free of the taint of passion, innocent of affection. They are complicit, they have an understanding. Theirs is a common task, speaking for the needs of the commonwealth, offering up their commonsense to guide the common people. An event has touched their common interest, otherwise Hooker would not have called on Hogg.

'Sit yourself, bailiff. My ears are open.'

'Gallimauf is dead,' said Hooker, pompous with news.

'I heard this told.'

'He hung himself.'

'Yes. What did he mean by it?'

'He did not say. He gave no goodbye. He left no letter.'

'He was ever vague and indirect,' said Hogg. 'In his death he completes the pattern of his life. We have lost a puff of wind. Though his gestures were always extravagant, their meanings were never clear ... Perhaps he was the fool I thought him – or else he sought to tease us.'

'There were some signs,' said Hooker.

'Yes?'

'He swung himself from the beam in his parlour. Beneath his dangling feet there lay some silver coins. In his right hand, clenched tight in his dead grip, he held a polished kettle. He wore his best jacket but no trousers. The parrot was perched upon his shoulder.'

'It is a powerful perplex,' Hogg conceded bewilderment, 'and I cannot decipher it. The solution may never be found.

But if it is discovered, it will cost a wealth of words and exhaust a sensible mind.'

'There's more to tell. When we entered the parlour and found him, he was rotating. He went clockwise two turns, then reversed this bias. The parrot looked at us and spoke. It was uncanny. He had the tones and phrases of his master.'

'What did the bird say?'

'He said, "Feed her sheep. She died for us," then spoke no more. If he knows the truth, he is not telling.'

'He is a devious bird and obscure as his master,' said Hogg. 'I never liked him.'

'They were facetious words at the time of sorrow . . . and puzzling. They wrap the secret in enigma, then shroud it at the heart of mystery.'

Mistress Hogg brought them tea. She stooped and shuffled as though weary. She snorted softly and gave a sly smile, all the time scratching her thighs.

'Your family is well,' said Hooker.

'Family?'

'Your daughter.'

'Alas, Cordelia . . .' Hogg paused, smearing a sudden tear with a doleful hand. His voice was burdened by sentiment. 'Fate has slapped her harsh. To leave her family for murridge, then lose her spouse so sudden and cruel. First he leaves her, then he parts entirely – bequeathing no estate.'

Both men fell silent. Hogg stroked the balding fleece upon his lap, flicking the loose hairs to the floor.

'The Lord Iffe treats her well,' said Hooker. 'He favours her above all his maids. She has a room for herself by the garden. It overlooks the lake. She has been given three aprons and two dresses all for herself. No heavy work is required of her now she is big with child.'

'It is a great sorrow that her husband should rest with her such a brief time yet still give her child. We pray that the infant will not borrow from the features of the father.'

'The people still remember,' said Hooker. 'Some copy him.'

'Yesterday I came upon three of them, conspiring in a tree.

All had grown beards . . . They spat down at me, shrieking as I passed. Were it not for my bearers – who are devoted to my person – they might have had me and seized me down.'

Hooker leaned forward confidentially. 'On Sunday some were missing from church. It is them. All are known and counted.' He drew a sympathetic and reassuring hand along the merchant's thigh. 'We will trample the outrage else it spreads.'

'Sir?' Hogg's voice quavered his confusion. The bailiff now stood poised above him, stroking his scalp.

'Your hair, sir,' Hooker explained, easing himself on to Hogg's lap, 'it is very soft.'

'Yes?' Hogg flushed with pleasure at the unexpected compliment. 'And yours too, sir, is most pleasant to the fingers.'

'In your ear, Clovis . . .' Hooker peered intently, 'there are little, curly, springy hairs. Does it tickle when I blow on them?'

And so they sat together, wrapped in their innocence, grooming each other contentedly until the room was quite dark and sleep came upon them.